In the great tradition of gaining life experience before embarking on the quest to write fiction. Brien Cole began working for Mildara Wines, Mildura in 1978 as a vineyard hand. Vineyard hand became cellar "rat" for Brown Brothers Wines Milawa 1982 which became Vineyard Manager Stonier Wines Mornington Peninsula 1989 and ultimately Winemaker (and general everything) Kings Creek Winery Mornington Peninsula. He has been making wine on the Mornington Peninsula since 1997.

Brien's first trip to France in 1982 saw him helping out on the vineyards of San Guiraud, Languedoc, France. In 1991 in Castillon, Bordeaux, and in 2010 a vintage in Saint Emilion, Bordeaux France. The "Lost Wine Degustation Society" has much to say about these travels.

In his quest to write fiction Brien published his first story in *Tabloid Story* in 1975. His first collection of short stories *Morning Parrot Trees* in 1979, which was republished in 2018 as *Still Life with Allen Keys*. Two novels, *Tiger Wolf* (2019), "Solero" (2020) and a kids book *The Adventures of Top Hat* appeared in 2022.

The Postcard from Madeira reads:

"When all is lost
Far out at sea
Reach for a Madeira."

It was written in sparkling gold "texta" and posted to Mathew &
Flinders Wine Merchants, Fairhaven, Victoria by Georgia Best (attorney
at law.) Thus beginning the private joke which would become the less
than private "Lost Wines Degustation Society."

Also beginning this novel featuring the customers of, staff of, family and
friends of, the shop, Mathew & Flinders Wine Merchants. Wine folk
all, with tales to tell. Tales of places sun drenched in wine. Beach side
cafesand Languedoc hills. A novel about friendship, love and longing,
exploring the concept of belonging in this country, in this town and in
the "Lost Wines Degustation Society."

The Lost Wines Degustation Society

Book One

A Postcard from Madeira

BRIEN COLE

ETT IMPRINT

Exile Bay

First published by ETT Imprint, Exile Bay 2024

ETT IMPRINT
PO Box R1906
Royal Exchange NSW 1225 Australia

 ISBN   978-1-923205-18-5 (paper)
 ISBN   978-1-923205-19-2 (ebook)

Cover art by Brien Cole

Design by Tom Thompson

for Malenka

"The wine lost... The waves drunk!

I saw extraordinary figures

Leaping across the bitter air!"

Paul Valery

A Postcard from Madeira

The message from Madeira was written sparkling gold "texta" and read.

"When all is lost
Way out at sea
Reach for a Madeira."

It was signed, Georgia Best, Member, Lost Wines Degustation Society. And addressed to, Mathew & Flinders, Wine Merchants, Fairhaven, Victoria. It was posted from Funchal, Madeira and is of oxen dragging a barrel.

1

The Lost Wines Degustation Society

The Lost Wines Degustation Society to which Georgia claims membership is a joke, (a long-winded joke) Matt's joke. The society consists of no more than a cork board nailed above some wine racks on which postcards are displayed and a list of wines "Lost Wines, lost to time" to which everyone who cares can contribute.

Madeira begins the list at least in Mathew's eyes. The list is not complete and the descriptor "Lost" debatable. There have been many debates between Mathew and Georgia Best, between Mathew and Baz Lehman and between Mathew and Madison Golightly.

Madison Golightly (Maddy) works with Mathew at the Mathew & Flinders Wine Shop on Saturdays, some Sundays, and Fridays. She has done so for years while working her way through a Visual Arts degree at R.M.I.T. Madison inherited her job from Mathew's daughter and Madison's best friend, Onna. Madison Golightly has fierce black dreadlocks, a nose ring, a tattoo on her neck of a Welsh dragon. She brings, she says, "Glam to the joint," with her "sixties" throw-back wardrobe courtesy of St. Vincent de Paul's and the boutique in the old Fairfield Mechanics Hall. Madison Golightly loves four things about the Mathew & Flinders Wine Shop and her job there.

The first is the postcard wall with the postcards sent by their customers from anywhere and everywhere. Anywhere and everywhere, they find something interesting, a wine which might be, could be, should be, on the list of the lost wines of the world. The second is the coffee machine, the coffee cups, the table on the street front overlooking the bay and the boat harbor. The coffee is gratis. It is not about the coffee; it is about the conversations.

"Our customers are our friends, we encourage them to sit, to chat, to share a coffee, a story or two."

The third are the vignerons, brewers, distillers, restaurateurs who frequent the shop and commission her artwork. "Why would they not?" She is quirky, amusing, humorous, fun, everything Mathew is not. "Okay,

Mathew might be Quirky," but she is Quirky in a sixties groovy way. Mathew is "Mister Time Warp."

The fourth is the town itself, and its peninsula surrounds where her family farm (Poll Hereford and Angus beef.) The town bordered to the east by the bay and the boat harbour to the south, southeast by the ocean straight, forming one half of the bay entrance, the better half. In its heyday Fairhaven was quite a town, the Melbourne paddle steamer berthing at the harbour wharf, and Melbourne society came on down, stayed in the guesthouses above the cliffs. Mathew's Grandmother on the Jewish Leske side built the big house which overlooks the harbour during those regal days. The elegance of the town died a slow death, once the paddle steamers no longer sailed upon the bay. Fairhaven was forgotten, a forlorn bayside town when Mathew arrived back to the town and the house his grandmother built, that slightly down on its heels Fairhaven suited him town, slightly archaic, lost to time.

Mathew owns a fountain pen, a fob watch (Madison didn't even know there was a word for a strapless watch, let alone that one existed) an anachronism of an anachronism, in her eyes, both Mathew and the watch. And then there is the list; "The Lost Wines of the World". These are the wines that Mathew's Great Grandfather would have sold in his fabled wine shop, Leske & Best Fine Wine Merchants. Mathew has a photo of the old shop, a sepia photo of another time, lovingly preserved and having pride of place on the postcard wall; Leske & Best, Fine Wine Merchants, Collins Street, Melbourne. (The Paris end)

The list of the Lost Wines of the World includes.
Fino, Amontillado, Manzanilla, the sherries of Jerez, Mathew once drank with his granny.
Banyuls, a fortified grenache from Collioure (where Dufy painted) on the French Spanish border, Mediterranean side, Mathew has been there only once, changing train track gauges on the French, Spanish border.
Muscat, Setubal, Constantia, Frontinac, Rutherglen, the great liqueur wines of the world.

Semillon, this is Georgia's addition, and it is debatable, the great white wines of Graves and the Hunter.

Malmsey, grown on Madeira, and many of the islands littered around the Mediterranean and Atlantic.

"It should include Mathew's Sparkling Shiraz," or so says Reggie Flinders, the Flinders of Mathew & Flinders, but Mathew said, "You are joking Reg."

Reggie wasn't joking.

The postcard wall sits above a rack of Mathew's own construction, made of wooden wine boxes framed in Huon pine. There are six pack Penfold boxes, First Growth Bordeaux boxes, Chateaux Haut Brion, Chateaux Beau Rivage, Chateaux Cristian Veyry. The postcards above the boxes roughly correspond to the boxes and countries below. Mathew collects boxes, even of wines he doesn't stock, boxes from Spain, from Portugal, France and Italy, but not from Greece, New Mexico or Georgia and only a single box from Hungary. There are holes in this world, Matty muses to Maddy. Ditto the Postcard world, for while their customers love to travel, they don't necessarily either travel to or send postcards from those longed for missing places.

"We will have to go to some ourselves."

It begins a familiar talk of places they would like to see, the wines of legend they would like, once, just once, to sit and sip in the land where they belong. It's a genie in the bottle type of game, one wish, one wine, from any place and any time. What would you choose, Mathew?

"*Vinho da Rodo*", every time.

"*Vinho da Rodo*" the legendary wine that's circumnavigated the globe, a rough translation. *Vinho da Rodo* epitomized the wines the world has lost to time. A wine which belonged to another age, the age of exploration. Grown on the Isles of Madeira which at the time was a first stop around the world, and not truly around the world, rather to Goa, to Malacca, via the Cape and Mozambique the empire of the Portuguese. It said something about the wine that they used the full barrels for ballast. Splashing about in the hold of a Square-rigged Caravel, to weigh the dam boat down enough to sail around the Cape of Good Hope, and back to Belem harbour. On the harbour quay they would empty out that bloody wine, from around the world and back again.

The wine once it had returned from rounding the world though tropic heat and doldrum air, the wine which had splashed and spilled through Atlantic storms and presumably been sampled, all the way there and back. That bloody wine, by rights, should have died at sea, what happened instead was a miracle, a wine transformed by heat and swell, a legendary wine is born and a wine forever tied to the age of oak and sail.

Mathew told Maddy, "I have a bottle on the boat, not of *Vinho Da Rodo*, a bottle of Madeira "Rainwater", it's sort of my token gesture to another age."

"Of course you do, you wouldn't be Mathew without those quirks of yours."

Madison Golightly has her own lists, but not lists of obscure wines, no one except Mathew remembers.

Maddies list looks like this:

a. Things I like about myself.

b. Things I'd like to change about myself.

c. Skills I'd like to master.

d. Qualities I'd like in a "husband".

e. Reasons for putting the word "husband" in inverted commas.

f. Why I would like to tell Mat that there is a reason his wines are lost, but I won't.

She likes Matt. Matt was born into the era which she should have been born into. Madison would have been "Fab" in the sixties, whereas there is no conceivable era of history where Mathew could have been "Fab".

There is one thing and one thing only to which her and Mathew agree, actually two, they both love this town and this tiny part of Victoria, and they both agree that wine must be from the place it belongs. Where that place is they will debate constantly, a Riesling from the Rhine, a Riesling from the Clare Valley, does a displaced Riesling truly belong in its displaced geography?

There are wines of place and time, stripped bare of affectation, the wines of plastic tablecloths, of villages somewhere in the Mediterranean, a restaurant terrace from a Raoul Dufy postcard and Mathew and Megs or Madison or Onna sitting on the terrace sipping wine which sings of stone and sun, and olive and pine, of pale white villages and fishing boats quayed.

"Waiter! calamari and a bottle of wine", a golden wine, with amber hints something captured in its soul, hill herbs and salt, and a slight sniff of cypress and wind off the sea.

2.
Juliet de Courmartin introduces herself

(Our occasional first-person narrator will try to explain what she considers inexplicable)

I am Georgia's daughter. Georgia Best, the one who wrote the postcard from Madeira it's important that I tell you, Georgis cannot be trusted not with the truth, none of them can except me.

I am as it were your compass, to navigate this world.

You can call me Jules, not Julie, whether with an "I" or a "Y" I will not answer to it. Juliet in French, but only in French because I am half French and the French language is gendered. I am therefore half gendered, don't think of that as a joke. And don't expect adjectives. I don't do adjectives, messy descriptions or the subjuntive tense. Not from me, you will get enough of that from them. Yes them, the "Society" the non-existing society they have loosely formed, and which they claim a membership, even me when it suits me. I told you I am honest, what more can I say.

Indulge me while I digress just for a moment on that question of membership, lose or otherwise. The writer believes this is a book about wine, it is not. This is a book about belonging. Who belongs in our little "Lost Wine Degustation Society?" Which wine belongs in the category of, "Lost Wines of the World?" End of my digression, let me introduce my mother.

Name; Georgia Eloise Best.

Born; 1968, August the 27th.

Weight at Birth; five pounds eleven ounces.

Weight today; sixty-five kilograms.

Height; five foot seven, according to her imperial self.

Hair colour; Blonde (Naturally).

Skin; Fine.

Teeth, perfect (expensively so).

Singing voice, soprano.

B.M.I; 20.

Heart rate; 120/70.

(Draw your own conclusions).

Likes; sailing, skiing, Saturday afternoons at Mathew & Flinders Wine Shop, Mathew (which she will not admit) French regional cuisine (but not haut cuisine) the music of Claude Debussy, the books of Anthony Saint Exupery, the poetry of Apollinaire, (note Apollinaire is not French).

Loves; me (a biological imperative) Grandpa's farm, her substantial accomplishments.

Dislikes; My inability to form lasting relationships, but not I guess her own inability. The slow strangulation of regional towns, regional wines, regional lives. The French language spoken badly (by me), the wines of Bordeaux made badly.

Disloves; my father (who is nowhere near as bad as she thinks.)

Member; Lawyers Union, Country Party of Australia (Lapsed, both party and membership) Society of Lost Wines, invented by her and Mathew. I'll tell you now there is no such society, but if there were it would look something like this:

Host, Mathew, wine merchant

Secretary, Georgia Best, Lawyer, and consultant.

Historian, Kato Brewster. Lecturer in history of Oceania (and wine Tasting.)

Assistant, Madison Golightly. Artist, and my best friend, also Onna's friend.

Winemaker. Baz Lehman, his parents farm abutted my grandparents farms.

Sales rep; Honda Magazaski (AKA Two-Stroke) He has a thing for Madison.)

Reggie Flinders; Mathew's business partner and part time savior.

3.

Georgia Best, an introduction.

Georgia Best knew her family name was significant from a very young age. She didn't know why. On the farm her grandfather had a Furphy tank on which was written: "Good, better, best, never let it rest, until your good is better and your better best."

Georgia Best took this massage to be her personal motto. Many times, and in many ways she wishes she hadn't. Good would have been good, better would have been better, but Best was her name and Best was her nature.

At the age of sixteen Georgia was strawberry blonde, tall, elegant, sophisticated beyond her years, she had skipped teenage gawky, jumped over the "Tom Boy" muddy, hurdled the innocent girlish phase and landed fully formed as Georgia Best, Head Girl, Chilton Grammar School. The girl with the notebook, tasting Grandpa's wine. (By way of explanation a different Grandpa from Mathew grandma wine tasting, plainly. However Mather's ancestral wine shop was called Leske & Best for a reason.) The girl was in a hurry at school, at play, in holiday work on Best's Great Western Vineyard. (Family name but alas no longer family ownership).

Melbourne University, Arts Law, where Georgia had a map of Paris on her share house wall. She knew exactly where she would live when she got there which Metro she would take to the Embassy. She'd work at the Embassy. She had it planned, every move, every step, every chance encounter. The French lover, the chateaux in this case on the wrong bank of the Dordogne, her first miscalculation.

Not so much the French lover as marrying the French lover, Philippe de Courmartin, Juliet's father. Banker, Chateau owner or more correctly member of the de Courmartin dynasty who own Chateau Haut Rivage, Bordeaux on the river Gironde, unfortunately the wrong side of the river.

It was rumoured, unfairly that Georgia married Philippe for the Chateau wines. Georgia didn't, she did divorce him at least partly because of the wines. The wine, Chateau Haut Rivage simply wasn't the "Best" it was far from best. It wasn't even the Best it could be, and when Georgia tried to improve the chateau wines, she discovered:

a. Australians know nothing about wine.

b. Australians are the scum of Angleterre. (He swears he never said that.)

c. Philippes aristocratic family has been making this wine in this way for seven generations.

d. Australians have no passion, neither in wine nor in marriage.

"Chateaux Haut Rivage, thrives on passion."

Chateau Haut Rivage, does not thrive, it survives, and "Yes", she told him that the way his father makes wine, the way his grandfather made wine, his great grandfather and himself. That way, is a lazy way, is a complacent way, is a way steeped in tradition, a tradition of hubris, and little more.

And so it was that every fight began, and every fight ended, until the last, and never once would Philippe accept, Georgia had the right to an opinion.

Georgia Best came to love and hate Philippe de Courmartin with an unmatched intensity.

Georgia Best loves and hates French wine with an equal venom. There are in her eyes two Frances, the inner preoccupied, vain, and delusional France and the modern, dynamic France. Never would she be able to separate her relationship with either, nor with Philippe. There is also she knows a third France, the vanishing France, the France of White Bordeaux. White Bordeaux, the Semillon of Graves, the first wine in her thoughts if she was to write, as secretary of their society which she is not, the encyclopedic "Lost Wines of the World." Which she isn't.

Georgia Best sent the postcard from Madeira to Mathew's shop. She should have sent it to Megs, Mathew's ex-wife, (how many times does she forget the "ex") and Georgia's friend. Megs will appreciate the joke at Mathew's expense. Mathew will not.

Georgia Best was thinking of Matt. Georgia Best thought about Mat more often than she would care to admit. Georgia has known Mathew for a very long time since they worked together over the summer holidays. Georgia was eighteen, Mathew was twenty when they worked at Great Western Winery, dragging hoses, cleaning tanks, shoveling marc and cleaning, forever cleaning. "Cellar Rats" the bottom of the winery pile. Mathew, Georgia, and Baz Lehmann, they all were good friends, if she remembers right, and she does, she always does. Mathew was at the time a moderately handsome man. Not her type, still not her type. However, Georgia Best does not have to be her "BEST" around Mat, or Megs, the advantage of very old friends. It remains true with this present Matt in his "Couta boat" shorts, in the afternoon sun, sitting on a bucket, some rigging in his hands. Matt is a bucket sitter. Matt sat in exactly the same manner on an upturned bucket next to the Great Western red wine press, fiddling with hose fittings. In fact, it was a familiar refrain in the winery, if you couldn't find a hose fitting, Mat would have it. If not in his hands, then under his bucket.

Mathew at least is consistent. And it partly was because of Mathew and partly because of Megs, that Georgia brought a holiday house in the town, joined the Couta Boat Squadron. She sailed the best boat while Reggie and Matt floundered about in the slowest.

4.
An Imaginary Atlas of Mathew's childhood
Both wine and people belong to place.

Mathew has always belonged to Fairhaven.

Fairhaven harbour circa 1969 (In photochrome) Mathew is in a boat, rowing imaginary waters. His boat has "Not been named yet and it never will." It is Mathew's boat and has a Sea Gull 3hp motor which rarely works, therefore the rowing. Dip and pull, dip and pull, Mathew, loves the boats on the harbour, the scallop boats tied up along the fisherman's wharf, the yachts near the breakwater, riding the bouys, the fishing dinghies smelling of whitebait, seaweed and fish bones. The shrill sound of the rigging, tasseled in the wind, or perhaps a P&O liner distant in the channel.

It is a strawberry day. A strawberry ice cream day which drips, drips, drips through the cracks in the wharf. Strawberry ice cream smudges the bay. The water so slosh, slosh about on musseled pylons beneath, bubbly, bluefully, blueishly blue. Jellyfish floating tentacle tight.

Great Grandfather Leske, Grannie's dad, Mummies' grandfather, and Mathew's what? Imaginary companion, spirit of the old house, ghost? Great grandfather Leske died before Mathew was born. The man not the stories, there are many, many stories all told by his grandmother, Evelyn Onna Gandy (nee Leske).

"My father (Mathew's Grandfather) was a millionaire, for a day, a week, a year, and then another scheme began, be it gold, or sugar cane or mineral water, or something equally extravagant. He travelled, travelled all the time, to all those old gold mining towns selling wine and brandy, beer, but always on the lookout for his "El Dorado." One day away, it's just there, underneath this coarse grey soil, a "Welcome Stranger" waiting. What a family to belong to, schemers and dreamers and takers of chance. "Oh, this family was something!" Grandma Leske said with pride.

Granny sighed as she admitted her youngest daughter (Mathew's mum) married down. She from the best school, she had a beau, lost tragically. She married someone else instead, didn't want to be the girl left behind by the tide of war. Mathew's mother brought Mathew to the old house with his sister and elder brother on most school holidays. Summers were best. Grandma had always liked Mathew. The strange lad who likes to sit himself on window seat with her husband's binoculars, looking at the ships pass by in the bay. Grandma thought he was nearly a Leske, the dreamer not the schemer, no head for money, yet an adventurous soul.

Grandma Gandy (nee Leske) never said a single word to disparage her family. They were something grand in this town, then. This town which slowly died with Grandma and continued dying, house by house, shop front by shop front. Skinner's produce store closed down, they boarded up the doorways and they took the shingle down. They closed the Bank of Victoria, the post office and the rural school. Some folk think that Mathew was the "canny" first buyers of the town's gentrification, Mathew thinks he was the last of the locals. Skinners produce store became in turn a surf shop, a gallery, a be-spoke furniture store and finally an epicurean organic food store with cafe-restaurant. The Bank of Victoria a cafe, antique shop then Gallery, the old Post Office a teenage hangout, a second-hand store. Reggie's mother's boutique for older ladies became Mathew & Flinders Fine Wine Merchants, a partnership and friendship which saved Mathew's life.

Grandma died when Matt was twelve, and with her, Mathew's beachside holidays, the old house sold, split unevenly amongst her children in the old tradition. Uncle Benjamin thought it best, he had a scheme; they would invest all the proceeds, it can't go wrong, in true Leske fashion it could, and it did. Mathew swore an oath he would buy the old house back again, maybe he swore it to himself maybe to his imaginary Great grandfather ghost, even Mathew is no longer sure.

5.
Georgia & Mathew, Interactions, Intersections.

Mathew was both infatuated with and intimidated by Georgia Best. Georgia is a class above him both in birth, Western District Squattocracy, intelligence, and sophistication. The fact that she likes him surprises Mathew, the fact that she doesn't like, like him enough, doesn't. Georgia Best, in his eyes, but not hers, should not be on the gantry of Great Western Wines, in dungarees and working shirt. Mathew had never seen her dagging sheep, tossing hay bales, or rounding up the mob on a dirt bike. Georgia would shake her head. Mathew was the sort of bloke who thinks a pretty girl just can't do this, break her nails, sprain a wrist, "Crickey he's a moron." Georgia Best just shrugs. Georgia's father, Earn Best, grew her up to think, there ain't nothing she can't do. Earn moreover thinks Matt's okay, "smart enough, a worker too, and he's honest no small thing. Not the lad for you my lass, but I would give the lad a job, just not give that lad, my daughter."

Georgia Best had thought the same. Best male friend, best male mate, best man perhaps no more than that. In Georgia's best life you cannot have a lad like Mathew, drift about, no grand direction, no grand plan. No grand vision just a vague, "what's next?"

There are girls in "School" for him, good girls who will love him for who he is, solid Mathew, a little odd, who looks back on a past that's gone. The past is over, the past is gone, yes Georgia's family once owned this cellar, vineyard, farm. Once Mathew's family sold their wine but that connection doesn't mean that much to her even if it means too much to him. *"Tant Pis"* as the French would say, won't be long before she's there, in France. While Mathew will be lugging hoses at Great Western or someplace else. Married to some girl from "School" who Georgia will introduce to him to. Georgia Best did not know but Mathew had already met her.

6.

The girl in the red one-piece (1984 Summer of)

Georgia Best and Megs had met Mathew in the same year, the same summer, the same week. Georgia on fermenter gantry Great Western Wines, Megs on the Fairhaven harbour pier, they thought the same thing as each other, and concluded very differently.

He was scruffy.

On the fermenters in working garb, ratty shorts, and wine-stained shirt, he needs a haircut needs a shave. He smells of sweat, she doesn't mind. Honest sweat, her father says, a man should never be ashamed of that, I'd rather a man who smells of sweet, sheep dung, cow flesh, dieseline than one who smells of office. Georgia had no time for those who didn't pull their weight and more, Mathew was a worker, nearly handsome, smart enough. He caught on quickly, yet even so Mathew was never more than a "nearly, almost, not quite there."

On the pier in the same shorts, a patch sown over arse, shirtless, a blue towel draped wrapped around his shoulders. He needs a haircut and shave as well. He looks kind, honest or nearly so, smart enough, and who wants more, and handsome, yes, he's handsome. Megs who is ruled by different gods applied a different ruler, "nearly, almost, not quite there, becomes I want to know this boy, what makes him who he is today and who he'll be tomorrow."

Georgia Best has a list, a checklist, bares no compromise, Megs an intuition.

Megs Rosslyn is day girl at that snobbish school, her sister went there, her mother, aunt, a tradition in their family. Megs never truly did fit in, not at least with the richest girls, the ski trips to Mount Hotham, the European holidays, winter breaks in Port Douglas, tennis coaches, Royal Yacht Squadron membership. Megs mostly didn't care, she got on with the "Arty" girls, hung out in the studio. No local school would have those things, lithographs presses, complete dark rooms, pottery kilns and pottery wheels and then there was the hockey field. Megs always has and always will find a way to compromise, to make the best of what there is, not scream and shout for something else, not quietly whine about her lot. Meg will cut the cloth she is given. And Megs Rosslyn expected odd, it is what she'd known her whole damn life. Meg's G.P. father collected stuff. There is no other word, stuffy Scientific instruments, a barograph and microscope, glass cased scales, refractors and one x-ray diffractor. Her mother is the perfect doctor's wife, a true alma-mater of the school, yoga, watercolour class, painting workshops trips away with the ladies "*en-plein-air*" and the appropriate charity.

Nola Rosslyn saw in Megs the talent which she didn't have, the form, the eye, the subtlety. She should have understood the girl, it rather went the other way. Sage advice to not let it derail your life, a woman does not pursue art, it is a hobby, can be no more, art is decoration.

Nola Rosslyn was a "Chilton" girl, presentation above all. A misfit like Mathew is not the boy, she would like to see her daughter with. A slightly misplaced awkwardness as if his body doesn't fit or he doesn't fit his form. He is wearing shorts, the arse is patched, wrapped in a somewhat threadbare towel, no shirt, no thongs, barefoot on the wooden slats covered with discarded fishing hooks, not an act of bravery rather foolhardy actually. He hesitates to jump off rails into the tempting azure blue.

Margaret Rosslyn (forever referred to as Meg's) didn't wear bikinis; "they don't flatter me, and certainly don't flatten me." She described herself as "chunky." Megs should have more flatteringly had described herself as "classic." She had just dived from the railing of the pier with a gaggle of friends yelling her on. The dripping ice-cream pier, the strawberry ocean forever pier.

She dared him to follow her into the brine. (Dared him to do a lot of things.) Megs had always told these girlfriends from school, "I'm going to have adventures, I'm not the sort of girl to marry the first boy I see." That first boy was Mathew, the one who reluctantly followed her into the brine, not with a dive but an awkward, wayward plunge, breaking Megs and her girlfriends conversation of dreams and careers, boys and glorious, glorious futures. Megs joined the boy on the lower landing.

Megs and Mathew talked. He wasn't she knew, the most handsome of men, above average, it's true, except for his eyes, the gentlest of eyes. They chattered. They chattered about dreams, about this town, what it meant to him, the holiday house on the cliff top which once belonged to his grandparents, his love of that house, this town, this pier and the boats which ride on the bay. He'd always thought he'd go to sea, except for his eyesight which is poor, so he has chosen to attend Agricultural College. "It's about horizons."

Megs who would begin Arts College that year understood horizons. And understood rather unexpectedly that they would navigate towards that horizon together. After College, after she'd graduated and was posted to teach in all places, Mildura, out in the desert, the red bare land of Drysdale, Boyd and Co, they had a group of friends, art teachers who picnicked on desert sands with brush and pen and easel.

7.
The Many "Where's" of Wine and People.

Mathew Radcliff is not a Leske and Georgia occasionally uses his real name to both remind him and annoy him. In Mathew's eyes he is a Leske, always preferring the German Jewish name of his grandmother and would have named the wine shop Leske & Best, except Georgia wouldn't let him. "You are not using my name. And I'm a lawyer."

Georgia does not think Mathew would make a good Leske, agreeing with Mathew's grandmother that Matt is too much the dreamer to warrant the noble Jewish name. And anyway, Mathew is not the true owner of the Mathew & Flinders Wine Merchants; that is Reggie.

Reggie is the Flinders of Mathew & Flinders. Reggie owns the building amongst many, probably more than half of the shop, certainly more than half of the couta boat, which was Reggies grandfather's. Reggies Grandfather was one of the original couta fishermen. Reggies boat is one of the original boats. In another very different way Reggie himself is an original, a one of a kind, a character, an institution, and an "old fag", (a Captain Haddock complete with dog Snowy). He is undoubtedly Mathew's financial if not spiritual savoir, a claim he would never make. Reggie is not a wine person, he buys once a week a bottle of "Captain Morgan Rum" from his own shop and has a good sit-down with Mat.

A Brief Interlude about Couta Boats.

They were working boats, refined by decades of chasing barracuda fish in the bay and beyond the heads out into the wild, into the ocean, into the Straight. A sturdy working clinker boat, the clipper of the fishing fleet. High in the water with a Gaff rig a long bowsprit to take a large jib. Beautiful boats which slowly decayed in boatsheds and mooring, on blocks in old yards. Rediscovered with the township some years ago, preserved and restored, by the "Newbies" in town. Depends who you talk to, a good or bad thing, Mathew has a share in Reggie's Grandfather's boat.

Madison Golightly: would be the first to observe, this fictional and real society, is not just a society for Mathew and Georgia's mates it is also a society for her contemporaries who happen to be their bloody kids. Madison Golightly, her best friend Onna, daughter of Matty and Megs, who although never married are (not) married now, courtesy, according to Matt, of Uncle Benjamin Leske's scheming and dreaming, and according to Megs, due to Matt's naive stupidity. (It's complicated.) As is counting Onna as best friend rather than Jules. Jules de Courmartin, Georgia Best's daughter, half French, on her father's side, complete Aspergers. They all went to "the school" as had their mothers. Jules is difficult, she is a rationalist, a researcher, a girl of ambiguous sexual leanings and terribly self-contained. Onna is Onna, a little lost, a little confused, but actually fairly okay with that. She has her mother's practicality, and some of her father's dreaminess, not too much, thank the Gods, one Matty is enough.

And while she is loath to admit it, she will include Honda Magazaki (Two-stroke, what else) Maddison's NOT, definitely NOT boyfriend. "He's keen on you!"

"Plainly."

Two-Stroke, does not ride a two-stroke, fortunately, nor does he ride a Moto Guzzi Le Mans which would be "FAB". He rides a Honda, of course, and is fun to be with, has contacts everywhere on account of his work in sales and because he is one of those guys. And neither Onna, nor Mathew know why he isn't her boyfriend when the answer is obvious, "because I am an artist."

And then there is Zak, Reggie's son from a brief and unsurprisingly, unsuccessful marriage, unless you count Zak as a surprising success, and no one really does. Zachariah Flinders is tall, thirtyish with spikey black hair wearing an old Ramones T-shirt and leather jacket which once was his father's.

Zachariah Flinders does not pretend he is easy to be with if anything he plays on the opposite. "I'll not make excuses," then proceeds to make some. His mother is undoubtedly and unhappily mad, not simply for thinking she could be married to Reggie, but pathologically so. Reggie says she is, was bipolar, amazing to be with, disastrous to be with. And Zak, well Zak is a chip off that block. He has a love-hate relationship with both of his parents; sometimes he hates both, sometimes he loves both (rarely) and sometimes he loves one and hates the other. Mathew, of course, has tried to employ him. When Zak is good, he is very, very good and when he is not; a disaster. He fights with Maddy. How can anyone fight with Maddy? (She is so cool.)

He fights with Madison, always Madison never Maddy, because;

Madison Golightly is pretentious. (She is only playing with the "cool" get-up, he says.)

Madison Golightly has no taste in music. (She doesn't rate the Ramones above the Violent Femmes.)

Madison Golightly is too much under the influence of Matty when it comes to wine. (She doesn't agree that if the Ramones made wine it would a. break all the rules and b. be fantastic.)

Madison Golightly is not angry enough. (Actually, she is not angry at all, and she is sorry that Zak is too angry.)

And then there is Kato who is older than Mathew, but younger than Madison. Kato worked with Matt in the Highton Wine Emporium while he was at Uni. He describes himself as a social anthropologist, a Kanaka descendant trying to understand his place in this Anglo world. He is also a wine educator, and a part time lecturer in Oceania studies at the regional university. A good customer, and good friend to Matthew, who he inevitably calls "Bro."

And not quite finally, but finally enough, Baz Lehman. Baz is a scruffy man, his hair perpetually sticking out in odd directions. Baz hasn't shaved, yet he must shave sometimes as he doesn't have a beard. He might hide himself on shave days that has always been a mystery. He dresses as scruffy as he looks. Baz Lehman started the Navarre Winery while still working with Mathew at Indigo Wines. He wanted to be, "his own man." Baz's Grandpa owned the land, which not incidentally borders Georgia Best's family farm and the old Navarre Quartz mine once owned by Alexander Leske. (Victoria is a small state and these coincidences are surprisingly common if you dig deep enough. So best not to.) In his own lackadaisical farm boy way he wanted to make a golden triangle rich red earth wine. Baz does not often come down to the shop nor come to Mathew's Society dinners, he does when he can, if he can get a slot on a crew sailing Coutas in the bay.

8.
It's a big ask

The Lost Wine Degustation Society very nearly didn't include degustation. It only did so after Mathew persuaded Megs (ex-wife although we are all confused) who was understandably ambivalent to be hostess of a dinner for Mathew's shop.

An early summer dinner, twilight hour, lights strung up upon the old oak tree, table beneath, overlooks the harbour pier, wafts of seaweed, kelp, iodine, sea salt fish, mingled with pine resin, frangipani flowering. A dinner, the first dinner, for those who have helped, those who we have known, those whose custom we value most, a wine shop dinner and so would like more, and Mathew would like Megs to help him.

They are sitting on the Yacht club deck overlooking the harbour pier. Their pier, the pier on which Mathew met Megs all those years ago. There is no place in this town that's not written into their history in one way or another. Even the deck of the Couta Yacht Squadron, which is relatively new, still it's better here than at Mathew's house which ironically is not his. The house is in Megs name, "we should change it." They never did. It will go to Oona, whoever's name the house stays in. They never finished sorting out the entanglement which is their lives. "We are Schrodinger's cats us two, in two boxes, don't open lids no one knows what you will find."

Megs is staring out to sea where one of Matty's liners sails, slowly, boastfully between the bouys, the bay a Derwent pencil grey, blue grey the colour which bleeds into sky. Megs loves that colour with a smudge of clouds just another twist on grey. Whatever markings on the funnel of the liner sailing passed she cannot discern, she would need Mathew's Observers Book of Ships to know. The Observers Book of Husbands is not out yet.

Mathew doesn't understand. Mathew doesn't get it." It's not always easy doing this, not as easy as it looks, sipping beer in the sun underneath umbrella, early summer in a cotton dress, favorite summer hat and he still looks at me, in that exact same way. He still sees me, in the one-piece bathing suit, he sees me as I am as well. He sees the woman sitting here, and many, many, many more, asleep upon the Spanish train, painting in the South of France, six months pregnant on the cliffs, painting boats, the lighthouse, sea and clouds, fluffy grey white baking blue. Both boats and clouds it seems to her leak the exact same colour. A "gun flint" colour Matt would say, describing both the look and taste, in the mixed-up way he does, although he pretends, he doesn't.

Today is toffee, bitter, sweet and very hard to navigate. Mathew isn't quite as clueless as she thinks, Just not so good at using words to describe the things so deep inside; the wave smell, back wash, rip tide, swirl, how can you pin a word to that, forever tastes flow in an out. He knows he broke her trust, broke her heart and messed things up and however much he apologized, it don't change a single bloody thing. He did it, full stop.

Let us plan our dinner. Let us plan a homage to another time, another place. It will be good for both of us. Matty says to Megs, and while Megs thinks it could be fun, old friends, new friends, everyone. She will have a role to play, a little definition, it makes the night much easier, step inside a familiar role, and one which suits the "Chilton Girl" old school, same as Georgia.

Mathew would like Megs to help him, Megs knows more about the food. Mathew will ask and Megs will say, "Yes. I will help, it actually sounds like fun." And even if Megs didn't always like Mathew, she always liked fun.

"What are you pouring? Gigondas, Muscat a Baumes de Venice perhaps, the wine is your thing, but we have to match."

"Let's start with Amontillado in the afternoon. I don't want to pour the obvious."

"Amontillado where you started Mat, with your grandmother beneath the oak."

"Chestnut Teal in memory of our Merbien days"
"Those days painting on desert sands, yes they were wonderful."
They clicked their glasses at a plan, "to us."
Meg's will say as a single word, "to-not-us."
"To-Not-us today!"

9.
Amontillado in the Afternoon.

Georgia Best was first, of course came to help make bouillabaisse. "Soupe de Poisson, actually." Georgia couldn't help herself, had to be her pedantic self, "This is fish soup not bouillabaisse."

Georgia's new beau, Travis Loyd (temporary status at best) arrives with mussels, prawns, and South Australian oysters. Temporary but certainly splendid in blazer jacket, dark hair greying swept back off a deeply tanned and handsome face. Poised and charming, (always rich), why bother if they are not. "It's not mercenary," she emphasized to Matt.

"Its a delicate balance Matt," Georgia says, "I don't expect you'll understand. I want to share things with this man, travel, dining, the yacht club of course. I'm not pretending this is a 'soulmate' thing, maybe I am delusional."

"Travis," she adds, "loves his wine, I thought he'd enjoy our dinner."

"I thought," she whispered to Mat alone, "you could use some corporate clients, he'll be a good one, a little conservative albeit, maybe you can broaden him. It's good to have a challenge."

Travis is English, home counties, he's been out here for thirty years but talks like it was yesterday he stepped onto Australian soil. It means that he is conversant with Jerez and has holidayed on Madeira. In fact, he sailed there from the Isle of Wight. It's enough to persuade Mathew but not Megs who says, "Matt, I'm pretty sure our Georgia likes to choose the kind of men she will never, ever fall in love with. There's a safety in their charm which doesn't ask too much of her. It makes sense but little else."

Onna doesn't like the charm of him in her youthful, self-righteous way. Claiming she knows them well, the parents of the girls at school. The men who own the Couta boats that she and Reggie are working on in Reggies boat house by the sea. Reggie employs Onna, who is not just Mathew's daughter but has "the touch" with wood. Reggie has never seen anyone as good. Reggie who is always polite to nearly everyone, he finds it best. Took an instant disregard to Travis. "He is not my type," Reggie winks at a private joke to Helena hanging on his arm. No one exactly knows for sure who would count as Reggie's type, (outside of Mathew.) It doesn't matter, Travis prefers a true, blue water boat. Travis will not waste his time on the younger folk except perhaps the pretty ones. So not her or Jules or Madison (though Madison is rather swell, behind the dreadlocks and piercings), although Travis would never see it.

Travis does notice Siobahn Kato's wife when she arrives, worth a "chat up" worth a "flirt." Her disturbing other worldliness. Siobahn is a Celtic girl, she of unknown quantity. She is taller than Kato. Lanky even willowy with unusually palish, porcelain skin contrasted with a mass of red brown Medusa hair. Kato always said she has a slightly otherworldly look, a look of faie, but exactly which Celtic faie he couldn't tell, of the sea, he suspects. They are of the generation in between, Megs and Mathew and their kids. No kids themselves, Megs has wondered why, another conversation. Not tonight, tonight is wine and food and tales told.

Goldie (a Californian Girl and slightly younger than Siobahn) arrived in classic surfer mode, salt crusted, clumpy, gorgeous hair, tanned and glowing (no other word.) Travis was fascinated with a girl who makes wines, who learnt her craft working in the Napa, Porto and Bordeaux. Making wines in an old surf shop, how appropriate she says, and sold by Mathew, or soon will be. Goldie has brought one of her wines, a Grenache, an experiment. Just one barrel "I'm not yet sure. I need to get to know it."

Onna had come with Jules, happy to have a meal with Dad, "Lots of Booze and things to eat, not so much for Vegan Jules." Georgia's "Aspie" daughter, who may allow her rules to stray. "For that is also written."

"What is written Julesy girl?"

"One should not insult the host." Jules has been reading the Koran again. "As an atheist." She says, "I need to know the moral basis of life on earth. I refuse to not believe in things I do not know about. I would truly like to know what quantum quirk of chemistry leads to our illusions."

Onna does not engage. Long experience has taught her not to, don't encourage, don't engage it's not just best; it is the only way. She's not yet drunk enough to follow Jules' pedantic reasoning. They are here to help and not argue about esoteric quirks of quarks, or quarks of quirks; Jules alone can tell you.

Onna needs Maddy as a foil, who is coming but is as usual late. Arriving "not with" Honda Magazaki aka "Two-stroke" just at the same time on the same motorbike. Madison isn't here yet: the problem was she was supposed to bring the hams and cheeses, olives, figs, stuffed peppers and Chirico from the Melbourne market. Caught in freeway traffic perhaps, found a pub or friend or something else exciting. They arrive together, on the back of the Two-Stroke's Honda 650 but "NOT TOGETHER, because we aren't!"

Baz Lehman's here driven down from the farm to stay in his beach house, probably sail, on Sunday if you need a crew. His wife Carol has always been something of an enigma but not in the Siobahn way.

"Carol is simply quiet, nothing more, a country girl who has never been too comfortable with people who she doesn't know."

Megs is empathetic. "You guys get to talk your wine, wine and travels, travels, wine, not so interesting to those who think wine is a drink and nothing more; let's get pissed together."

Reggie and Helena; "Our own Diva." Georgia says. Helena Rubin, Prague refugee, artist and singer, lives in the Europa Apartments; in the penthouse she likes to say, overlooks the harbour. Helena, her flamboyant best, dressed in fashion of the "Prague Spring" circa 1968. She comes on the arm of Reggie Flinders as she always does. Reggie her great companion who sings bass tenor, Gilbert and Sullivan Light opera Society. It is how they met.

Helena always effervescent in her high soprano voice.

"Darling I can't imagine how; the man can run a shop at all. Look at what's he wearing, oh my God! Is he actually wearing that, has he just stepped off a boat, and not the sort of boat I'd board."

To Madison another screech, "Darling, Darling," Helena says "You look so good in those scrumptious clothes. If only you were shorter dear, I could dress you wonderfully. You are not afraid of clothes my dear. It's so European." There is no higher compliment. In Helena's eyes, the Europe of her younger years, the Europe of her glory days. " Ah! La Strada", she would sigh. "That was when the world was right. "

That the world is no longer right is of course a given. It cannot be you understand, a country should treat its artists well, they bring so much, more than just their art, they bring colour to a world which wants to fade into shades of grey. "The world needs you my Madison and your wondrous clothes." Helena has her circuit; a promenade every morning, every eve, which begins at the cafe Emporium. at her table during breakfast hours. "Bring me my pastries and coffee, Joe" and the paper; he knows which one. Every Friday afternoon she'll pass by Mathews if there is something worth my time but you must always tell the truth, I won't stop by for just anything."

Zachariah Flinders last to arrive with a bag of chips and bigger attitude, with a swagger. "I don't care," and particularly to whatever Madison thinks. Who he avoids judiciously. Talking to Reggie "Dad" beside Helena who fortunately has stopped enthusing over Madison. Helena is in love with youth. Zak is young enough to count.

"Pose is style misunderstood." According to Helena, who hugs Zakariah close to her and whispers, "My darling boy, she is just a girl whose trying, alright too hard you say but don't make it harder than it is. It's a girl, a boy and nothing else."

Zak jives about the subject.

"Tell me Helena, tell me Dad, what will you two sing tonight?" They had promised they would bring a song and Zak has brought his key-board. Zak has no interest in what they decide, he knows the songs they love to sing. Opera Buffs; perhaps the only music worse than Maddison Golightly's choice is definitely his fathers. Zak takes a glass of Amontillado from a smiling Two-Stroke who likes the girl, it is quite extraordinary. Two-Stroke asks Zak about Mathew's sparkling Amarone Shiraz which Zak helps Mathew make or more precisely Mathew helps Zak for Zak has largely taken over. Two-Stroke doesn't ask the normal questions; what he is doing with the fermentations, or in the vineyard. Two-Stroke is only interested in how Zak is selling the wine and if he has any ongoing plans. "Have you thought of revamping the label?"

Amontillado the first of the wines in honour of Matt's beloved Grandmother. What they once sipped right here beneath this very old pergola, an ancient mission vine ensnared in crumbling wooden lacework.

Amontillado, cheese and ham, crusty bread and tapenade.

Tasting Notes; Amontillado;

Colour. The colour Mathew acutely notes is the exact same colour as Goldie's hair a light ethereal golden grain infused with salt and bleached dry straw.

Nose. "Wet pebbles in the sun." Georgia Best will not be outdone. The straw green apple is obvious as is sea spray just a hint of rotting seaweed on the beach.

Palate. Intense minerality (wet pebbles) lemon, salt, clinker boats "according to Onna", the slight dusty smell of wool, Grapefruit, dried herbs

Amontillado is about chalk and the Atlantic coast, a property it shares with Madeira, Constantia South Africa, Setubal in Portugal.

A Brief and improbable explanation of straw.

Amontillado is a straw wine.

"The technique is ancient, Homer wrote about it, and it was probably ancient then."

What we know; ripe grapes are laid on mats of straw, or hessian sack, to dry in the southern European sun. Or laid on racks in northern barns, (think of Amarone) concentrating flavours, concentrating flaws, for everything's a two-way street. Sun burnt sugars will give us, a treacle kind of caramel, a slight residual sweetness. Drying grapes upon the mat a sponge of any scent around it, be it aromatic trees, cypress, gums, or coastal pine, be it meadows, adjacent fields, all the signatures of place and season as well as grape. Be it grenache, muscat, palomino, or malmsey. Amarone or Banyuls, you can taste the raisining, the intensity of shriveled fruit, a long and grand tradition. If the grapes are ripe enough by raisining upon a sack; they will create enough alcohol to stop the fermentation leaving some residual sweetness. Mathew thinks that is just half the story, it also allows some oxidation. It seems improbable but it is essentially how it's done, allow some oxidation of the wine. These wines were made long before the advent of bottles or of cork, shipped by sail on rocking seas in earthenware amphoras or wooden barrels. We are only guessing after all but Matty suspects it was the only way to preserve the ancient wine, to gently let it madeirize, (the word taken from the wine.) The process requires an intense wine, a wine which would retain its flavour, high in natural alcohol, high in sugar and robust enough to allow a little oxidation. No flimsy, modern table wine would ever meet that challenge

Amontillado followed by Grenache; as Megs predicted, Mathew will pour a Gigondas. While Baz Lehman has brought his Navarre Grenache to compete against Mathews Gigondas, a Rhone grenache with a touch of Shiraz, Mourvèdre. Just a touch to allow the Grenache to dominate with all its sappy, luscious fruit. liquid fruit pastilles, berry fruits, cherry, plum, raspberries and violets.

Baz Lehman's wines are unfiltered, and unfined, purposely so. "Why would I rip out the guts of my wine, to make a clean product. These are farmer's son's wine, a little bit rustic, a little bit course but precisely the flavours which come off his land". According to Baz you can taste the rocks, taste the gum trees, taste the good Pyrenees air, sunshine, summer storms and all in between. If you want to taste wine that is clean, that is fine, that has been immaculately groomed don't buy a Baz wine or Goldie's she adds.

Baz Lehman is famous for lack of a comb, for a beard unruly, for holes in his daks, for dirt on his hands and a gruff sense of fun. What you get in the man, you get in the wine.

"I give you Grenache, both going solo and with a whiff of Shiraz; just a whiff mind you Shiraz will dominate if you give it a chance. Grenache the Leporello to Shiraz's Don Giovanni, the workhouse, the belittled servant. You know it is the most planted vine in the world. Enough of this chatting. Let's drink some dam wine." Madison Golightly pours everyone a glass of each wine.

Baz knows his vineyard, each row of vines, each tilt of country, shift of ground, he knows how soil translates to wine. "It's curious, but also true, that the grapes I grow from here to here, (not even a complete row it seems) prefers the oak of central

France, while adjacent rows prefer Allier, the oak of Alsace, northern France. It takes many, many years to know a vineyard as well as that.

"I can do it," Baz Lehman says, "because I'm both vineyard hand and cellar rat, two tribes, you know, they rarely speak, you'd think they would, they mostly don't. I call myself a cellar rat, it's half a joke, and half a truth. Winemaker, vigneron, I don't know? I'm just the guy who presses grapes, runs the ferments, cleans up the marc, fills the barrels, chooses the barrels and chooses when to take wine out. It is a job of many things, many small decisions, a job of judgements in the end, let us not pretend it is more than that. I am a farmer in the end, the end and in the beginning."

Two-Stroke will take Goldie aside, introduce her to Baz and Maddy, "Here is a plan, Goldie makes her delightful Grenache, from Baz's Fruit. Maddy does the label. Good for Baz, good for Goldie and good for Maddy. "They'd be perfect for each other, each whacky in their own way." It's what Two-Stroke does all the time joins the pieces, conduits the meetings, intuitively knows who fits whom. "Let's discuss it later."

Baz's Grenache versus Gigondas; old world, new world facing off.

The consensus is Baz wins on Fruit, they expected that, but the Gigondas has something else, a touch of pine and mountain herb, a backbone of chalky tannin.

"Terroir" says Georgia," is not just France being esoteric, the taste of landscape seeps into wine, the smell of trees and herbs and grass, the taste of dust and rocks and air and I suspect the taste of sunlight seeps in too."

Matt has always known it does. Even the moisture seeping in, there is something sodden in *Cote de Beaune* which is never found in *Cote du Rhone*, further south along the river Rhone. A reflection of heat on rock, a very subtle smell of chalk. it's a different kind of dust than Baz's gold field gravel.

"Which matches better with the lamb?" That's a better question. Baz brought the lamb down from the farm, slow cooked in Provincial herbs adding to confusion. It asks another question, which is the point.

Matty asks, "to what extent do wines belong in the region where they are grown. Wine belongs to Place, neither wine nor poetry can ever truly translate".

"And what of people", Kato asks, "can we ever truly translate?"

Kato Brewster understood. wine comes from somewhere. It has roots, literally, into the bedrock of the land. He knows it's true. It is true of Kato; he comes from somewhere or many "wheres".

Kato knows what Matty's saying but, belonging is not a simple thing, belonging's not a this or that. Belonging is complicated, by the manner of your coming, freely or forced, who was stolen from their lands, or left without a choice to make. Kato Brewster appreciates the connection between wine and place the occasional magic of some island café terrace, the Mediterranean Sea below. There is a larger history. It's something Mathew should understand, the story of the boats at sea, bringing cuttings in their hold. Those same holds would also bring a human traffic to work the fields, to Matthew's beloved Madeira. There is always more to know, underneath the underneath, what of Sete and Frontignac, what of Marseille, Collioure; don't get nostalgic for places you have only glimpsed the surface off. Look at the faces of your friends, Helena, our own refugee, Baz and Georgia, squatocracy, Two-Stroke, Irish Japanese, (As if that's even possible). Kato Brewster a child of the Kanaka trade. The Leske family, escaping what, pogroms, wars, Reggie Scottish fishing folk forced out by the clearances many stories weaving in and out, many threads, and many lives.

Mathew understands what Kato says, he is just a bit confused about the many wheres of Mathew. The Jewish Leske just a name, his true name in his eyes yet he knows not much of what Jewish means or Jewish is. Great Grandfather Leske the last true link to lost Jewishness. Mathew don't know what that means.

Reggie, bored with talk of wine, begins again a joke he shares with Onna in the workshop building boats.

"Onna, I know your answer but what of Jules," Reggie says to both of them, "What kind of boat do you think you are? One that's painted by Pommard, floating on a shining sea?"

Jules considers this question truly worthy of some thought. "I would be painted by Paul Klee," Jules answers, "on a sea of raging squares. I think my mother would like to be a Pommard boat but that's not her, she is the "Cutty Shark." The first departed, first boat home, leave the others in her wake. Mathew would like to be a Caravel sailing out of Belem wharf, but actually I think he is the boat, undescribed in, "The Hunting of the Snark." We, it's crew. And Megs, yes Megs our Onna's mum, there are two Megs, the lifeboat Megs who keeps us safe, and the private Megs who paints. The private Megs is a Dufy sail upon a distant horizon. Siobahn the Lady of the Lake doesn't need a bloody boat and Kato is a war canoe, with the fierce pride of his lost race. But it's not the boat which interests me, in your quaint illusion, what I would like to know Reggie, is the nature of our sea."

"Our sea is wine," says Maddy, "It's why we are here. What unites our diverse crew."

Underneath pergola, autumn sunlight, dappling, a faint rustle in the leaves, and new configurations. Georgia with her handsome beau, sits with Baz and Carol a little contingent of the volcanic plains. Leaving Megs to sit with Matt. Reggie with Helena our most stylish queen, princess of strong opinions; about wine and men and art but not too many about boats.

"Amarone," announces Matt, with a bell of spoon and glass, causing Jules to laugh out loud, "see he is the bellman!"

Amarone the best and last, placed in line before desert. Amarone, rich and dense, a syrup as much as it is wine, Christmas pudding fruit, dark red plum, vanilla, chocolate and cocoa, pepper smoking tobacco edge, open up discussion.

"Argue forcefully amongst yourself, what is lost and what is gained by concentrating fruit like this."

"It has changed the aromatics," Jules is contemplating the chemistry in the glass, "It's very slightly caramelized, just a hint of burnt toffee. I can't describe it but it is there."

In her daughter's stout defense, Georgia, says, "when we were young there was a jam, in a can if I recall, and on the top, there was a skin of fruit and sugar, I fought my sisters to be the one to open our jam can and steal this thin, delicious layer, for me that's Amarone."

"It's time, it is time!" he rings again the Bellman's bell or clink of glass.

"A song," says Mathew, "Let's have a tune, let the night end upon a song, sung by our own one and only Diva. Direct, or nearly but close enough, from the famous La Stata, our Helena."

Three cheers erupt, as everyone has had enough.

The promised song will be sung by Helena, Reggie accompanies.

Helena steps onto the makeshift stage. Reggie is there beside her. Zakariah off stage right begins to play his keyboard. From Gilbert and Sullivan, the Opera Buffa, from the H.M.S. Pinafore "Things are never what they seem":

"Things are never what they seem
Skim milk masquerades as cream
Highbrows pass in patent leathers
Jack draws strut in peacock feathers"

"More," they clap and request again, it is traditional they know, an audience has obligations.

10.
Mother and Daughter by two.

One.

Megs is stacking up the plates, plates and glasses, and the rest, helping Georgia, but also Matt. Onna asked her mother once, why she did this, why she helped, what dam reason can you give for playing host with Matty.

"You know Darling, it's actually not the problem you think it is. Of all the things this is the least. I would feel far less if I was just another guest instead. And mostly these are common friends, good to catch up, share a meal. I have a role, a part to play, a rhyme, a reason, for heaven's sake we all know Mathew could not do it. He is good in the shop, was good amongst the barrels, rambling on about the wine. About the places we have been, the things we have seen together, we were together all that time, Languedoc and Bordeaux."

Two.

"It doesn't make you happy." Jules says to Georgia.

Daughters are like that, they know you too well.

"You are happiest Mum, down at the beach, it's time you slowed down, be a little bit less than best, don't be forever the mother who is driven relentlessly on."

Georgia Best, a little bit of Georgia Best, knows it is true, and some of Georgia Best knows Jules is trying to evict her from her own house and retire her to the beach. Daughters shouldn't be like that, she has read the manual on daughters, but Jules wasn't in it. The good daughters, the rebel daughters, the pleasing daughters and the princess daughters but not the unemotional, pedantically rational, intensely curious, narrow band daughter who is Jules. The daughter who never wanted any sort of girlie-best-friend mother but might have preferred, a mother more present, a mother less driven, a mother she could share, in an intellectual way, some of her obsessions. "I brought you the good things," too much of an "Aspie" to really want those.

Georgia had often observed too much of her father had come out in Jules. It's hardly her fault but what looks good in a man, isn't as flattering on the face of a girl, the nose just too slender, makes her eyes narrow in, a chin without a perfect structure of bones. It would be better if she knew how to dress but has adopted the uniform of feminist chic. She does it to annoy her, they both know she does, at least partly. And then there is her manner such complete disregard for all social graces and the art of small talk. Mislabeled in her mind, nothing small about talk which facilitates conversations, helps others to warm to you. It has been noted, an impossible shame that the head girl Georgia, Chilton Grammar School, has a daughter who was very nearly expelled from the same school, except for Georgia's intervention. "You need her marks!"

"They asked me to leave. It was hardly my fault, they were teaching mathematics to parrots, Reggie's cockatoo would have been bored in that class."

She is, however, almost right, about the beach house, objectively, rationally, even financially, it made some sense. If she could let go, not even let go, maybe let slip, her tenacious hold on being the best. She is happier down there, amongst the bird shit and rigging, wearing boat loafers and her favourite hat..!

Grandmother Leske's Wine; Sherry

Palamino is the grape of sherry in all it's forms.
Fino, bone dry and chalky.
Manzanilla; Fino from the sea, the fishing villages of Sanlucar de Barrameda, with the slight salt tang and hints of white bait, fishing nets, quays.
Amontilado, aged finos, complex, and compelling.
Oloroso, dark, dense and brooding.

Also known as; Palamino Fino, Palomino Basto, Listan, Blanco Jerez, Chasselas de Jesus, Doradillo, Listrao de Madeira, Seminario, Winter Catalan, and many many more.

Flavour Profile; somewhat neutral but no other vine takes on quite as much the flavours of place, the salt air, the chalk soils, the distinct flavour of the Flor yeast, the mysterious element within sherry.
Growth Pattern; a vine with dark green leaves, long cylindrical and medium sized thin skinned berries. The grapes are juicy, fragile, only moderately sweet and low in acidity. Palomino makes a rather dull still wine but a perfect base to absorb the "terroir" of Jerez.
Soil type; bare white chalk coastal dunes.

The Seasons of Sherry

Manzanilla, the sherry of Sanlucar de Barrameda, the Atlantic coast, fishing boats in the harbour smelling of white bait and salt, sun and sky and summer. Grandma's favourite afternoon tipple, beneath the great oak branche in the beach house garden.

"Sit with me and share no more than a thimble, maybe two, taste your heritage my boy."

Manzanilla, a summer wine; it sparkles light, "My father said, each sherry has a season. Summer is Manzanilla's light, that golden glow of summer sun. Amontillado, it is autumn's wine, a tinge of brown and oche. Amontillado with a sense of time, departing, Oloroso winters wine, deep and dense and brooding, which leaves Fino for the spring's youth, young and fresh and blooming. My father had the gift of talk. How much was true, how much was not, I don't know or care for he filled my life with wonderous scenes."

Each sherry has a season; Mathew with his thimble full did not think then what he thinks now (there is a season for every wine under heaven.) Those vineyards have stood three thousand years planted by Phoenicians but who drinks sherry anymore. "Just me, it seems and only then in memory of another time."

Interlude No. 1; Leske and Best Wine Merchants (1863-1938)

Alexander (Zanda) Leske was more dreamer than schemer, who had the misfortune of believing he wasn't. In early manhood (as in all stories or at least the ones Mathew reads) he set off to make a fortune, make his mark, under his uncle's influence to plant sugarcane in far North Queensland, Rockhampton. Wrong land, wrong time, wrong place. He often spoke of his Kanaka friends, workers, comrades but never of the disaster which ensued. Alexander came back to the family firm, but he was always restless, always ready to take a stake in the next big venture, the next big scheme. Spritz water from Buffalo Springs, a messy beginning, equally messy end, but not the worst of his lunacies. Gold! How Alexander loved gold; Malden Quartz Pty Ltd, Castlemaine Deep, Mount William Gold and Navarre Quartz. He sold wine and bought gold mines one end to the other of the famed Golden Triangle although not so golden for Alexander.

A Handsome man in the photograph, up upon the mantle place, with a roguish countenance, and most extraordinarily wide moustache. Dressed in European elegance. "He was a European," Granny said, "He always was particular about that, born in Berlin, albeit by chance, the family was from Poznan. Thank God I am not an Englishman, he would always say, a European does not dress in dungarees and workman's shirts. A Central European man has culture in his fingertips."

"A great wine must be drunk from glass," Granny gave Mathew a tiny crystal glass to sip, Fino, Manzanilla, Oloroso, and spoke about her father. "My father was a millionaire, for a day, a week, a year, and then another scheme began, be it gold, or sugar cane or mineral water, or something equally extravagant. He travelled, travelled all the time, too all those old gold mining towns selling wine and brandy, beer, but always on the lookout for his "El Dorado." What a family to belong to, schemers and dreamers and takers of chance.

Zanda Leske never felt the same reverence for the family name; he was a Leske, the second son, Leske & Best, the family firm, his elder brother's firm in reality. He always was the restless one, looked here and there or another scheme, a way to separate himself from his brother, find his El dorado. His daughter's stories are not complete, some things left out, some things unsaid, some things they would never talk about. Not a devout man he would pray in synagogue for the day when he will find his El dorado.

He worked back in the family firm Leske and Best, Wine Merchants, Collins Street (the Paris end). And for his amusement (most of all) began a wine club for customers. Leske and Best wine club meet once a month, officiated by the very urban, very charming, and unusually handsome, Alexander Leske, immaculate in a dark European way. Folks liked him, folks liked to buy wine from him, liked his stories, his manners, his jokes (perhaps not his jokes.) He was an asset to Leske and Best. His older brother Isaac Leske was the strategist, the one to decide what to import, what to buy, what to sell and for how much. Leonard Best, the partner in the name was the nuts-and-bolts man, in charge of making sure products arrived where they should, the shop was stocked and orders came and went on time. Neither Isaac nor Leonard had the magic

Alexander had, to be liked, to have folk want to buy anything of you. "My mate Alex, did me a deal."

The Wine Club, or as Alexander liked to call it, Wine Saloon, in the best traditions of Berlin (his place of birth, albeit by chance.) The Wine Saloon was a place to educate, to illuminate, to intrigue, inspire and mostly enjoy the wine experience for a group of (largely) men from the city. Isaac's fellow businessman who liked to discuss gold mines, wool prices, opportunities in sugar cane, once bitten twice shy for Alexander, who graciously pours a welcoming amontillado while listening to rumours. He will learn of the latest mine, Maldon Quartz, they will learn to match an amontillado with pre-dinner salted herring.

The postcard from Jerez written in blue ink.

Straw gold matts
In Spanish sun
Holy transformation.

The postcard was written by Mathew but never posted, it was written to and for his grandma. You cannot post a letter to the dead. You cannot say, "I made it, Granny, Jerez, Spain, home of Manzanilla, Fino, Amontillado.

11.
"Chestnut Teal"

Granny said, "It's the only one, the only sherry worth its name made here in Victoria, made by Merbien Wines and sold in our premises, Collins Street." (The Paris end, near the Windsor, and Melbourne Club, not that the Jewish Alexander could become a member.)

In the heat of a desert town, on the bones of an ancient inland sea they grow Palomino, make a sherry worth its name and this is where Megs is sent, first year out of Diploma of Ed. To teach art to country kids. Mathew followed in her wake, in this indeed in everything. Mathew with a Diploma of Agriculture, Longerenong Western District, he should have gone to Roseworthy South Australia, but in a time before the boom, any qualification better than none. The boy at least is flexible will work in vineyard, winery, has experience, dragging hose, washing tanks and rouseabout for Great Western, they put him on, if not to make the Chestnut Teal at least to learn about it.

Mathew general cellar rouse-a-bout, cleaning tanks, cleaning bins. helping out as best he could. This is how we cut our teeth. Occasionally in the barrel room, washing barrels on the strip of concrete beyond the door. Washing barrels, a sort of swirl, a rocking, rolling swishing, fill the barrel just enough with the hottest water and begin to rock them back and forth, generate a swirling wave. In the barrel, a boat bilge churn then tip it out, refill, rewash and around again, ready for refilling. There is something about wood, at least that's what Mathew thinks as he churns the barrels. A boat like smell of oak and water, a familiar, friendly smell. Oak is forests green and rich. slightly damp on fungal floored. Oak is workshop shavings, dust, and the smell of barrel room.

In the barrel room the barrels are stacked three high on red wood planks. There is an overwhelming smell of wood and wine and muskiness. It's cool and dark, somewhat dank. Mathew didn't know that it should not smell of dank until many years later. Mathew liked the smell; the barrel room foreman liked the smell. The barrel room foreman, everybody called "Woody." It weren't his name but Mathew knew no other. A grizzly man, short and bald with a raging rouge red beard. and while Mathew didn't know it then, he was the last of a dying breed. Woody has a workshop out the back a cooperage with staves and rings and tools to tear apart, reassemble, repair leaks uncrack cracks, replace rings, barrel heads and splitting staves, oak shavings lying all about. They called him Woody, sort of funny, sort of not, He comes from South Australia, where they still make barrels " Don't you know." He'd been in that job twenty-five years, knew what he knew, how to run a barrel room. How to stack and clean and fill. How to top and rack and when. "When." he said, "one off the secrets to making wine is not so much the what, but when. The when to or the not to. Sometimes the hardest decision is to not do it, leave it alone, don't intervene, its doing exactly what it should."

Woody didn't say a lot. He described to Matt the shape of wood, the beauty of its grain and smell, "not all the same, if you know what wood is wood, you can smell the forest."

"You have to think that even then, he knew he was the last of those; the generation of people who could fix what has been broken. Repair the barrels, take them apart and reassemble piece by piece. Smell this starve, now smell that, that's the difference forests make, Limousine, and Nevers Matt, and see the grains they aren't the same, colder forest, tighter grain and tightly held, a secret smell."

Matt befriended the old guys, something about his "time-warp" self. They were the true teachers of his life. A snippet of the truth from "Woody" another from "Hoppy" Steward as bit-by-bit Mathew learnt from those men, the "old-timers" oft forgot.

12.

Pruning Palominos (Winter of 1989)

Mathew general vineyard staff works with the Old-timers.

Ian "Hoppy" Stewart wore a grey punter's cap smudged with the red Merbien dust; a cocky peacock feather tucked into the band. A St. Vincent de Paul suit jacket, grey, non-descript and ancient. He considered himself the most dapper of tramps, dressed in "satirical elegance". He would say and laugh a crazed, extravagant laugh. He had a laugh of a Sulphur crested cockatoo, raucous and flighty, bow legged and limping he would shuffle down the vine rows chuckling and talking to himself. Alcoholic, inebriate, raconteur, gambler, and liar. Hoppy may or may not have been part Italian. he claimed to be, he claimed many things not all of which could be true. He claimed to have fought in Korea, which probably wasn't true. He claimed to have seen Bradman bat. He claimed to have had been a Penciller for a famous Melbourne bookmaker who knew Squizzy Taylor. He had at various times claimed to be both a catholic and a protestant, Italian and Koori. That his grandfather was a riverboat captain. That he had been in turn a professional river fisherman, a bookmaker's penciller, a soldier, a gangster of sorts or at least and always disrespectable. He had one driving ambition; to qualify for the invalid pension and retire to the gold fields of Bendigo. Always referred to as the "invo" or "my own little Eldorado," because no one can live on the "susso". The only two things Matt was certain of, was that Hoppy had spent most of his life in Merbien and if you cut Hoppy his veins would bleed grape sap.

"There are three types of pruners," Hoppy claimed. "The hackers, they just cut. The pruners, pruners use their brains, they think about what they are doing, have an eye for shape and disease. And the budders, budders have a second sense, they know what the season is going to be like and they prune to the coming season.

Hoppy laughed. Hoppy's laugh was outrageous and contagious with an element of madness because Ian "Hoppy" Stewart was undoubtedly mad.

It was Matt who suggested he could work vineyards in Bendigo, in the off chance he didn't find gold.

Hoppy, stood back, looked hard at the boy, who he knew was stupid but didn't yet know just how stupid a person he was, "ain't no chance I'd do that, you know, gunna find gold, and anyway I'll be on the "invo" and have my gold lease. Those new vineyards, poor buggers, they don't know you can't run a vineyard without people like me, doing cash work on the susso, whose gunna prune, whose gunna pick? They'll never find people willing to work. Never find people with the right kind of skills not like Merbien, every picking hut shelters some old bastard like me."

Hoppy had the eye; he could see the cuts within the tangled mess which is all Matt saw. Hoppy saw the vine's arms he would leave amongst the tangle. Matty would never underestimate that skill, the simple beauty of it. The ancient Palomino vines had indeed grown old and tangled. The crowns of the vines from which new fruiting wood is sourced had grown or been allowed to grow higher than the fruiting wires such that the always brittle palomino canes needed to be gently bent down to the wires.

"Don't use that." Hoppy would direct Matt. "Do you see the cane underneath, cut away everything above it and it will be in a perfect position to lower the crown."

"One cut for shape."

"Two cuts to clear away the old wood."

"Look carefully, you can do better."

"Always cut for next year and always prune a vineyard you pruned before. Don't waste time correcting someone else's mistakes."

"The perfect cane doesn't exist."

"If the perfect cane did exist it would look like this; it would have buds evenly spaced the width of your fist apart, it would be as thick as your middle finger and would originate below rather than above the wire and just below it there would be a perfect spur to replace the cane the following year. Thinner canes are likely to have too many buds, thicker too few. And the buds per cane set your crop level on a cane pruned vine. Too few buds means too little fruit and too little fruit is bad for the grower and bad for the vine because a vine with too little fruit will grow too vigorously and that is bad for us, big bull canes are too hard to prune. So we make less money on the picking and less money next year pruning. Too many buds and the vine will produce a lot of small bunches, too hard to pick, we don't like that either."

"It is a just right Job."

"Just right" was surprisingly elusive for Matt, in spite of constant direction.

"Cut a little lower."

"The cane on your right is better."

"Always leave an extra cane in case one breaks."

It broke.

They pruned the Palominos first because they burst last and they want to prune last what bursts first, to delay their budburst beyond the frost. Therefore they will prune the Colombard last. We will leave forty buds, twenty each cane, evenly along the wire. Hoppy knows how to prune, he knows how to leave an even twenty buds either side of the crown, and he never counts. His finished rows are meticulous, precise and elegant. Matt in the next thirty-three years of viticulture would never meet a better pruner. The second best would one day be himself but he would never be a Hoppy.

Hoppy was as Hoppy said, "a Liberace of the loppers."

13.
Dominic Narboni (Pied Noir)

Dominic Narboni dark curly hair, Mathew's age or slightly older, fresh from the Stag's Leap, Napa Valley, California. Mathew will work with him on the presses, white drainers, red fermenters, a good job for a newbie kid, until they assess what he knows, and doesn't know. "Not Much," Dominic teases him. "He is not a winemaker, that's okay." Dominic's uncle worked the fields, carried his secateurs everywhere, felt naked without then holstered Western style, a viticultural Billy the Kid.

Two weeks before the first fruit picked, their job was to clean and clean some more.

"No better way to know your way around the equipment you will use." Ted Hazelgrove smiled at that; he'd been told the exact same thing God knows how many years ago. It won't hurt the boys to learn to clean the bloody stuff.

Seven stainless steel tanks with bases which slope towards a large hinged stainless-steel door, stainless screens inside, through which to drain the juice from skins. Juice, when they are draining whites, overnight just to extract "free run" clear juice gravity fed over to the tank farm where they start the fermentation. And wine when they are draining reds which have fermented in the tanks. The challenge, with either, is always opening that flaming door. Three fermenters held ten tons, while four held twenty-five.

Lift the screen, loosen the door, inch by inch, Mathew directs the flow of juice and sloppy skins, into the hoper of his pump, juice or wine, squirting out, cup your hands and direct it down, under pressure from twenty tons of juice and skins above. The first few minutes are the worst, depending on how well it's drained, sometimes a reservoir of wine is left in amongst the mass of skins, sometimes a tsunami of skins will overwhelm the door and pump, more often though the opposite, and someone, the someone who is always Mathew will go inside the tank and dig out skins while Dom controls the pump and watches out for Matt, least he succumb to CO_2 poisoning. (They say it is a pleasant death but not on my shift so says Ted.) Dominic chats with Matt, best to keep in contact.

They talk wine. They talk about the press, which Dominic can't believe, they are still using that antique thing. "My French rooster press," he laughs, "a Coq continuous screw press, in the South of France we still use those," but Dominic explains Mathew, "it is a bad, bad press." Dominic used the English "Bad" often and not always appropriately, his only explanation was, "in California they would not use a press like this, and in the South of France they would."

The continuous screw press (Coq is the brand name it has a picture of the French rooster embossed on its frame) is basically a large screw with ever decreasing screw wave intervals encased in a stainless steel frame. As the grapes move along the screw, they are pressed harder and harder both by the diminishing screw intervals and by a core of solid pressed grapes between the end of the screw and the press door. A continuous screw press has one advantage, it is as the name says it is continuous, you never need to stop. Modern presses you fill, you press, you empty, you clean and you refill. If you want to make exceptional wine you would use a modern "Air Bag Press." As Dom explains to Mathew, a continuous press is harsher, you have less control, and it pulverizes rather than squeezes the grapes.

"The South of France," he says to Matt, "is only known for its bad wine. In the hills above my town, I could grow a good, good wine. I think that is my dream to do, it's not impossible in Languedoc where land is not expensive and without the appellation rules a winemaker has some freedom."

If Mathew had a dream, and at that moment he didn't, it would be to make a wine, "My great grandfather could proudly sell in his wine shop." A famous shop he told Dom, the Paris end of Melbourne, a statement no Frenchman would ever understand and no Pied Noir would want to. To make a wine his ancestors would proudly sell, Dominic can understand. Dominic's English not quite good enough to understand nuances. "Tant pis" he says in French, he could help Mathew, he appreciates by teaching him the most important thing. How to taste. The free run juice, the wine in press tray, wine in tank, the fruit as it arrives on trucks, taste, taste, taste, but do not say. "I like this or I do not. Taste and ask, what do I experience on my tongue, in my mouth and on my cheeks, taste and remember, file away, this taste, this sensation, good or bad, every taste a lesson."

They talk of wine and talk of France and talk a lot of family. Dominic is not quite as French as you might think. He is, he says, a "Pied Noir."

"What the heck is that?" says Matt.

"My father is French, born in Algiers when it was France, not Africa. Africa took Algeria back and the French took us back, but reluctantly. France was not then a country of "many-somewhere else's." France did not know what to do with us, especially true of us black feet, part Sicilian, mostly French, some Berber crept in of course. Too African to be French, and no returning to Algeria. The rebels took our land, our livelihoods, we came "home" well home at least to my grandfather, if no one else"

To the town of Sete, the first port of call from Africa, a town of reputation, a port town of pirates, thieves, everyone has a game to play, and every shade of humankind. Dominic Laughed, "I grew up there, my companions a diverse mixture, in the army my comrades were fellow Africans and Islanders. So *tant pris* I have never thought like a Frenchman, it's why I know the South can grow wine of quality not just crap."

"The French believe in rules," He said, "rules of appellation, I have friends who want to be more French than French, to slot back in, only sometimes do I feel that I would like to be like them, mostly I think that I have a freedom, others don't, to only be French when I want."

Mathew's great grandfather was a European gentleman, born in Berlin, Granny said, a cut above the Englishman transported to this country. Granny exaggerated yet, Mathew has always felt this land, this place or maybe him, accepts too easily, that part of him which says. "Somewhere else is better". If that place be Bordeaux, Burgundy, Jerez; the part of him which says, "if I were to make wines I would make wines like those." When he knows if he had anything like his Great Grandfather's alleged swagger, he might say. "I can stamp this wine with an Australian sensitivity!" Its an old, old argument, both grape and folks have heritage. We all come from somewhere, even if that where has vanished, lost to time, or that's what Kato always says.

Vintage arrives, grapes come in from the fields on farm tractors, old red trucks and dodgy tandem trailers. Merbien Palomino; the ragged look of late picked fruit, slightly raisined, wrinkled skins, crushed to must and pumped into an empty ten-ton drainer. To the drainer they will add brandy spirit just enough to extract flavours from raisined grapes. It's an exact job, enough, no more. Ted Hazelgrove explains to Dom and Matt, "pure alcohol does not act the same as juice, it will extract different flavours especially from the raisined grapes. As a consequence, they must, "press the "be-Jesus" of the fruit to extract the sweetness of the raisined fruit and not waste the bloody brandy spirit."

Matt had told Ted and Dom about his connection to this wine which his Great Grandfather used to sell. Ted says, "Matt, I have always liked the family connections in Australian wine industry. We have employed a lot sons and recently the daughters of the First Families of wine. Darenbergs, Lehman, Browns and Campbells, Grants and Burge. In some ways we are a tight knit bunch, sometimes at each other's throats, sometimes have each other's back, just like family I suppose."

Ted did not elaborate; he has other thoughts and other fears that he did not think it would remain that way much longer. Even now the corporate world is knocking. "We need their money, we need their marketing skills, their connections or this company will be left behind. This company will slowly die on the vine as they say, in this case literally." He knew the arguments, they are sound, he doesn't doubt it. Just wonders what the price will be and what place he and they will have in it.

He told Matt, as one of the "old families of wine" he should take some time to see how we make our Amontillado. "I'll get Woody to show you around, the vats and barrels and explain our solera to you."

The Palamino grapes are crushed, pressed and fermented in enormous open wooden vats. The ancient vats are three times Mathew's height and roughly the size of a large, galvanized rainwater tank. They are says Woody, "the originals. Imported from Germany when the winery was founded."

They have added more brandy spirit before the fermentation uses all the grape sugar to stop the fermentation and leave just enough residual sweetness. Ted wants the wine to have enough residual sugar to balance up the intensity of the raisined fruit, the intense treacle flavours. The vat is open to allow the Flor yeast grow on top of wine. The Flor yeast while looking like a pond water scum is actually essential to the flavour of sherry. "The taste of sherry is largely the taste of Flor yeast, think of blue cheese without the mold" Explains Ted.

Dominic has questions which he needs Matt to translate not the questions rather Woody's answers for Dominic cannot understand a single thing Woody says. Or Sam on crusher, or Alex on centrifuge or any of the truck drivers. "Are they speaking English?"

"Of a sort," Mathew says.

"Then what does it mean, "things are crook in Tallarook."

"It's a bloody good question, hard to say."

It is Dominic who understood, this wine is not an Amontillado, strictly speaking. "No it's not, it is an Australian interpretation. "Why should Australian's not reinvent the wines of Europe," Dom shrugs, "Why not, I am African I don't feel obliged to follow the French Yes and No."

And; "Why he wonders in a town which sun dries every grape they grow, sultanas, gordos, currants, don't they sun-dry the Palamino, the one fruit which could benefit the most."

"It's a bloody good question, maybe they do in Tallarook."

"Then we should go there."

Ted Haselgrove climbed upon the barrel stacks in the old cellar, Woody's domain, extracting samples for them to taste. "The solera is as you can see is a simplified version. A true solera would have wine from every year, we cannot justify doing that in barrel costs nor storage cost, we store just the volume of wine we need and from the better years." He says to Dom. Not to Mathew, who is just a viticulturist.

A brief explanation of Solera

Solera; is a system of aging wine in barrels where wine from every year is retained in barrels, and the wine is a blend of a portion of each years wine. A small fraction of each barrels wine is extracted successively down the years until a product which includes every year of the Solera is included in the final blend. It is used in Spain in the production of sherry, and variations used in the production of Madeira, Muscat, Port and Vin Doux Natural. The simplified Merbien solera is a common simplification where only some older wines are kept in bottle to add depth and concentration of flavours to the young wines.

The Solera made sense to Dominic, who is fascinated by the older wines. The intensity of wines which have spent so long in older oak. "In Frontenac we make a wine from the Muscat a Petit Grains with a similar feel but not the intensity of this wine. This wine is not like a Frontignan though it which reminds me of a Malaga." (A Spanish Fortified wine which Mathew has never tasted.)

As they taste wines from earlier and earlier years the intensity of the wine increases, the oldest barely wines at all, more a treacle, syrup, a wallop of flavours in the mouth.

Ted Haselgrove explains to Dom, the art of blending in his view. "The objective is a balanced wine, a just enough wine, I like to say. Just enough of this treacle to form a sort of underlay, in music it would be the bass, in the background but always there. The ground on which you lay the rest, the tenor barrels not as old. The alto's have just a few years barrel age and the first and second sopranos, this and last year's wines which are the sky, sparkling and refreshing. Too much of one or not enough, and the wine would simply not be the wine."

"No," says Dominic, "it would be another wine instead, in Spain they would make three wines not one, a Fino from the freshest wine, an amontillado, which is what your wine is more or less and an Oloroso."

"Yes, and once we did, but this wine barely makes enough to justify itself to us, I think if Merbien Wines were sold, the accountants would summarize this is not a commercial wine. Too much blending, too much stock tied up in the ageing. I hope I'm wrong." He sighed and said, "At least we have it now, let's drink, to those wines which may be lost. To the lost wines or maybe those slowly vanishing from the world."

Barrel Sample, Merbien Wines, Solera.
Colour. black tea, walnut brown, moderate density
Nose. polished walnut, nuttiness, raisins, rancio.
Palate;. dried fruits, raisins, figs dates. Molasses toffee notes candied fruit, citrus peel, warm lifted alcohol.

A lovely wine, rich, evocative of autumn days the perfect aperitif or after dinner wine. And while it has nostalgia value, it also deserves a place on the modern Australian palate.

14.
Lake Mungo Shores (Autumn of 1990.)

Painting *en plein air* Lake Mungo, there needs to be a word for lakes that are lakes no longer. Non-Lake Mungo, desert edge, desert sands and salt crust shore Meg Rafferty and her friends from the art department. The Art Department *espire de coups*, Rod, his wife Francesca, Doc and his wife Lena (who like Mathew is not an artist), Mathew who brought Dominic. There have been many picnics, in which the three artists paint or draw. Lake Mungo, Hattah National Park, Murray Riverbanks. Pack some food, some wine, and drive out of town to paint and eat and drink and swap gossip of the school and talk politics and travel, where they would like to go, not been, galleries they would like to see, famous scenes they would like to just step into, although the moment gone when Monet, or Pommard, stood there.

One day maybe, someone would stand where they once stood. Would they eat as well as us?

Rod loved to eat, "who does not?" He has a European sense of "the table" pleasing Dominic who complains Australians eat like Englishmen. Rod is not an Englishman. He is Scottish, red hair, pale skin, a band of freckles above his eyes, a larger man, good humoured, a country boy, just not from here. Painting in Fred William's style, dots upon the landscape. Megs in her water colour paints the desert minisculia, a bleached and twisted tree struggling against the landscape. Francesca painting exaggerated colour, splashed across her canvas. Francesca, their Italian lass, short and nuggetty, a woman of strongly held opinions. Megs and Francesca, thick as thieves, in spite of differences in style and substance, of art and life. They have bonded over being here, first year teachers, outback town. Doc, the elder of the group, tells tall tales of his life, to everyone's amusement, perhaps not Lena, who has heard them all. Slender Lena, dark curled hair, fine featured, a Polish girl, the classic artist muse and girlfriend who is actually a gentle soul, according to Mathew, he should know. Mathew and Lena, the two non-teachers of the group, and therefore "chat while the others paint."

Lena had brought falafel balls. Mathew has brought a citric salad, Rod his famous curry.

Megs and Francesca are talking to Dominic.

"What is Desert in French?" Megs asks.

"Desert"

"Yes, desert."

"Desert is desert."

"Do you like it here?"

"Here in the desert or here in Australia? Actually, the answer is the same. The desert I like because I am out of Africa, Australia I like because in France there are too many rules."

It is very late autumn and vintage is over. They are sitting on a picnic blanket on the top of a massive and ancient sand dune on what was once the shores of lake Mungo but is now only the rim of an enormous basin. It is warm rather than hot, the sting having finally gone from the summer.

They are eating cold chicken curry and salad, drinking a Merbien Wines Riesling which Dominic says, is "Puh,,,,ordinary." Then adds, "In France we would not make this wine, not in the desert where it does not belong, maybe crazy French rules are not, quite as crazy as I think."

Both Megs and Francesca want to know about the village Dominic comes from, his life in France, not about Australian wines. They have had months to talk about wine.

He tells them of his South, Languedoc-Roussillon; the world of Dufy, Cezanne, Gauguin and Van Gogh, a world they know through paintings. His South is not so famous, the hills above Montpellier, the long escarpment which is the southern edge of the *Massif Central*. It's beautiful; sandstone buildings tiled in red, little villages, olive groves, vineyards, cellars, market squares. It's the France you all imagine. It's not he said as hot as here, this is more like Africa, Algeria my old home, the edge of the Sahara. It is savannah country, salt bush and mulga, sparse and grey and barring this ancient ochre sand-dune incredibly flat. It is not quite desert; the true desert is hundreds of kilometers further north. Mathew's pedantic, engineering father would make that distinction, everyone else calls it the desert.

Dominic said to Francesca, Megs, "If you ever come to France you should visit my village." He wrote his address on a sheet of paper from Rod's drawing book. Dominic's scrap of paper was their first destination in Europe.

15.
We Should Go

Megs lay on the bed propped up by two pillows wearing a slight cotton shift, pastel yellow, she smelt of Rosemary shampoo and sweat. She spoke excitedly,

"In one years', time Mathew, one years' time. We are halfway there Mathew. I want to see Europe, Spain and France. I want to see Italy too, of course. Monet's garden, Van Gough's South, Cezanne's south, Dufy's south. I want to visit the Pompidou Centre, see Florence, see Paris and Rome. Do I want to see Rome?"

She raised herself high on the pillows, so her legs curled out from the sheets and turned slightly to look directly at Mathew who was slumbered on the futon bed, still exhausted from vintage and not really wanting to engage in this. He rolled out of bed and walked to the kitchen to make morning coffee.

It is a warm, fragrant autumn day. A flimsy mist low over the bottom of the vineyard, the few remaining leaves yellow and orange on the vines. Somewhere a kookaburra is laughing and somewhere else a cockatoo screeches. The air clear and still and blue a perfect desert morning. Mathew makes coffee in the percolator. The New Guinea coffee smells fragrant, dense and tropical. Today he doesn't need to work, there are no grapes, no picking, no trucks or crushers. It is the making of a perfect day and the very first day he thought the thought; that there should be a word, with only one purpose, to describe the act of exploration of wine.

"Yes, we should go."

16.
Jerez Spain (Easter 1991)

In honour of his grandmother first stop is Spain, Jerez, sherry country, and then onto France, Midnight, quay light, changing trains, on a station, in the rain, the rain which falls mostly upon the plain, a bar open in this midnight hour. Coffee? Beer? Mat knew the word, his only word in Spanish. Take a table, rucksacks lay beside them. Two Malagas will warm us up, might help us sleep on the next train, which arrives too early in Jerez, they hadn't booked, they never do, hadn't factored in at all, Easter celebrations. Crowded second class carriages, they squeeze into a compartment, family move up and over, children asleep, politely moved and please come in, gestured more than spoken. Share some bread, share some ham, share some wine, the peasant kind, rough and strong and tannic. Megs upon his shoulder, snoozes or not quite it seems. Yes, she'll have a bite of that, a sip of the wine going around, will join a bit the gestured chat, half in hand and half in French, a default language in Matt's eyes, if anybody can't understand what he says in Australian, surprisingly it sometimes works. He will use it once again, trying to find a place to sleep in booked out Jerez Spain.

"Mind the rucksacks while I go Pension to Pension and find a room. Have a coffee, sketch a bit, this could take longer than I thought."

This is not the Matt she knows; he is never quite like this at home. At home it is Megs who takes the lead, a curious reversal of their roles, a welcome change if nothing more to rest upon his shoulder. Mathew loves the train timetables, the market haggle, Pension price, better in the morning, read the guide and plan the day, the week, and what I'd like to see. What I'd like to drink today, what wine was this town once known for, for Jerez it's Fino. Not the sherry we drink at home, Matt drinks, Megs corrects herself, but a dry wine, unfortified, young and vibrant, but only here. Only in the bars of Jerez de Frontera.

"But why do you come here today in the middle of the "Semana Santa de Jerez" there is no room available, in this house or anywhere." He took forever wandering, until he found eventually, a sort of closet understairs, "Don't even ask me what I paid.

Megs didn't.

In the afternoon they drank, in a café cobbled street, medieval old town other world. The wine they came here to taste.

Wine Tasting Notes; Jerez de Frontera, Fino,
Bodegas Carvey, Calle Guia Bar Juanito
Colour. Pale tournesol blush, incandescent vibrancy
Nose. Straw, dry, husky, faint chalkiness, dust and flowers, fallen petals and hay bales and dried yellow flowers honeyed hints of caramelized almonds dried apricots.
Palate. Lemony acidity briney dried Mediterranean herbs. It tastes like the hills outside the town.

In the evening, the town explodes with firecracker bursts and drums. Hooded apparitions in black robes, move through the narrow city lanes shouldering a wooden crucifix. A parade of wooden Jesus's held aloft by a crowd of hooded figures, Jesus with the wounded swords, Jesus on the crucifix, a golden Jesus on a bed of flowers. Pained and tortured Jesus is held high and proud along the lanes. Flowing towards the cathedral a parade of crucifixions amongst the firecrackers, candles burn, chants and incantations, clouds of incense swirl about through the crowds which gather. Here comes another Jesus now, held by purple hosts this time, in the hooded robes they thought were only seen in Southern States hiding Klansmen, for Matt and Megs it lends an edge of evil. In the land of *Auto-de-fae*, a swirling smoke-filled crowd of ghosts has a special haunting edge.

Megs will always associate Fino with the parade of Klansmen holding Jesus aloft above the swirling crowds. Mathew saw another ghost, dark and so familiar, Great Grandfather Leske, stories told, of his descendants who once were confronted by the distant ancestors of these men carrying their Jesus high. Searching through the lanes of old Jerez for the descendants of those who nailed their savoir to that wooden cross. Many, many years ago, it may be yet it happened. It's just a pantomime but with a deep and violent history.

Once upon a time you know your ancestors were burning here in the fires of Eater week.

Dominic Narboni's wine; Grenache

Grenache (Garnacha tinta, Grenache noir, Cannonau)
Flavour profile; red berry fruit flavours, raspberry, strawberry, confectionary fruit, fruit pastilles, pepper and spice, cinnamon, nutmeg.

Distribution; widely planted in Spain, Rioja, Aragon, Navarre, Southern France, Languedoc, Roussillon, Italy, Sardinia, Australia, McLaren Vale, South Africa.

Origins; possibly Tinto Aragones (red of Aragon)

Growing Habit; strong upright grower suited to warm dry climates and able to tolerate strong winds (Mistral). Grenache requires a very long growing season it buds early and ripens late, reaching high levels of alcohol making it suitable for producing fortified wines, notably Banyuls wines of Roussillon.

Soils; thrives on schist, stony soils, older vines yielding less fruit with concentrations of phenolic compounds producing darker more tannic wines.

Grenache most likely originated in Catalonia as Tinto Aragones (red of Aragon) from where-it spread into Languedoc and southern Rhone. It was one of the first varieties introduced into Australia. It is suited to hot, dry conditions and requires a long growing season. In southern France Grenache thrives on schist and granite soils. Older vines with low yields can increase the concentration of phenolic compounds and produce darker, more tannic wines.

Garnache in Spain. The low-yielding bush vines on brown schist soils make a tense rich concentrated and dark coloured wine with hints of fig and tar blackberry and dense dark berry flavours.

Grenache was planted widely in the first boom of Victorian wine; by the German's in Grovedale (German Town), the Italian Switz in Yandoit, Franklinford, the Rutherglen McKay's, the Great Western Bests. Leske & Best stocked many of these producers wines although to be honest Victorian Grenaches and Shiraz's, were really a minor part of their sales. Leske and Best sold brandy, rum, beer and champagne, (Mumm Champagne exclusively). Sherry and Port to finish a meal, a glass of Madeira to finish the port. A good wine shop, Alexander liked to say and he liked to think Leske and Best was a good wine, needs be a place where a person can find, the unique, the surprising, the gem in the shelves.

Maybe he said that, maybe did not, even if he didn't, it was Mathew's code. A Shop which sells the surprising, the unique, even the Lost Great Wines of the world.

Interlude No. 2 Wine Tasting Mathew & Flinders Friday afternoon. (Present minus twenty two months)

Honda Magazaki aka "Two-stroke" revved into Mathew & Flinders firing on all cylinders to ask immediately, "Is Maddy here?" in his explosive double-time voice. Honda Magazaki, wine agent for Port Estate, artwork by Madelene Golightly. He knows that she is. Friday afternoon tasting, of course Maddy's here. Two-stroke likes Maddy more than Maddy likes him and anyway Maddy did not want to discuss love, life or liaisons. This is a wine tasting, not a date.

They are tasting Grenache, specifically Baz Lehman's Navarre Grenache, various vintages with Goldie Reason. Goldie Reason, "Californian Girl" competed on the world surfing circuit, never quite made it but had the "look" they wanted to sell swimwear to a million girls. Goldie Reason's photo is still mounted upon the walls of the Jan Juc surfboard factory now the home of Goofy Foot Wines. Goldie found wine in Portugal, the land of sea, Atlantic coast. "You'd think a Californian Girl would find wine in the Napa, or the Russian River." Goldie explains to anyone who will listen, "I never do things the proper way. I am a goofy-footer, on the board or how I live. Goofy is the other way, that's the point of goofy."

Goldie Reason, in spite of her wonderful name, "the golden reason," doesn't necessarily think it through or apply the curve of logic. (She is the opposite of Georgia Best whose name dominates her psyche, her sense, her very being.)

They are tasting Grenache and discussing Artwork, Maddy's artwork, and Goldie Reason's wine. Hypothetical wine, hypothetical artwork, which Helena Rubin says, "Oh you must do it DARLING! There are too many boring labels."

"Too many boring wines." Goldie Reason is determined to do something different, do something unique, perhaps utilizing some ancient techniques, sack drying or "did you know in Banyuls they ferment wine in large glass demi-johns, buried in the ancient shist, cooled by soil, warmed by sun. Amazing, who invents these things?"

Kato Brewster agrees with her but has another angle. "It's not just wines which are lost. Mathew only thinks of the wines but it's also all the local knowledge which goes into those techniques. How would you know how long to leave the wines in the glass demi-johns. How deep to bury them? In what soils and at what ambient temperature? It's all the skills, experience, accumulated over centuries, passed from father down to son, given the era it was in it would have always been father to son. As a Kanaka I understand the broken threads of knowledge.

Goldie Reason reasoned that a variation on the theme, could, would be interesting. Baz's grenache with so much fruit, with all it's luscious, confectionary, melt in your mouth jamminess.

"If I made it, how about in a Banyuls glass demi-john buried in the earth or not, wouldn't that be something else. As Goofy-foot as it gets! It might even bloody work add another layer, another understory off tannic weight and tannic strength."

Goldie Reason revving up, bursting with ideas. "Fermented in ceramic amphorae, I have always wanted to play with those most ancient of fermenters, ancient technique new ideas. I am excited, "Goldie laughs, "it as goofy-footed as you can get."

The Good Bonbons of Banyuls

BANYULS-sur-MER — Les Vendanges

The postcard was from Banyuls. It was written in green ink.

Another old sack
Has buried its head
Into the good earth of Pyrenees schist

It was written by Dominic and sent to Mathew, it had one message, *"Why aren't you here?"*

17.
Saint-Guiraud, France. (Spring of 1991)

Saint-Guiraud, France, Dominic Narboni, assistant winemaker, Saint-Guiraud Cave Co-operative, for this is the socialist south, the south of bush vine Grenache, Cinsault, Carignan, Syrah. Mathew observes; takes notes, scribbles diagrams, drawings, in a Dalgety Seed catalogue notebook between May, June and August of 1991. Mathew and Megs have rented a small sandstone village house with a blue door on the street leading downhill to the square. The square where the old men of the village sit on the granite bench or upon the terrace tables in the evening twilight air, sipping pastis. A Hotel de Ville, Patisserie, Café du Midi outside of which terrace seats cluster under plane tree shade. Always old men beret capped reading Midi Libre, there are no young men in San Guiraud, or at least not many. Petanque on Sunday afternoon when the same old men in Sunday clothes are joined by comrades from St. Andre, similar men on leaden canes. Party comrades, resistance men, the Marie walls are plastered with Party propaganda, Francoise Mitterrand, *"On President juene pour un France Modern."* Only these old comrades would ever think of Mitterrand as young. Monsieur le Mayor a socialist, a brave man of resistance is a dark-skinned man with grey black hair beneath the ever present beret. The men's wives, including the mayor's, are short, often stooped and always grey. A waddle of village wives and widows who squabble at the market stalls every Saturday afternoon, scarves tied firmly around their hair, cotton bags are bulging.

The young are missing, they have gone away to Paris, Lyon or Montpellier. Dominic is an exception not the rule. A fact which is pointed out not by Dominic but by Francoise (Franny) Bregis, the English teacher from Montpellier and Dominic's friend. Franny wears Mr. Mago glasses which dominate her face, she has dark bobbed hair, and is a larger girl in every way, a presence, an energy, a light. Franny became their translator, friend and sometimes rescuer from French misunderstandings. It was Franny who explained to Mathew and Megs the workings of the villages, the cave co-operative and the vineyards, although she knew nothing of the wine, except, of course, to drink it. Franny did know how the men work in their vineyards. How the Cave Co-operative is structured along the lines of the socialist south and the social history of the village.

It was Dominic who volunteered Mathew's muscles, Mathew's arms and legs, and thankfully not mind helping out in the vineyard of his friend Claude Merchant. (In the black, of course, it is the South.)

The old vineyards terraced into the steep escarpment to the north of the town. A hotchpotch of shapes, squares, hexagrams, diamonds, triangles of every configuration. The vineyards are small, very small, some less than a suburban house block, none more than half an acre. They are mostly walled (or Clos) planted intensely, the vines one metre apart, the rows one and a half metres wide. They are not trellised rather self-supporting bush vines or supported by a single post when they are young. They are not generally young. They are as ancient as the men who tend them, some vineyards as ancient as the father's of the men who tend them. Old Grenache, Cinsaut, Cardinale, Mourvèdre, Syrah the canopy collapsing into the ochre soil. Backdropped by truly ancient olive trees, pin de montagne, oak. A villager may own many of these plots, although rarely together. As vineyards through the generations are willed and divided, too many sons or too few, marriages, births, deaths and conflicts written into the landscape. A villager may own a few, may own many yet however many it won't be enough.

It won't be enough to keep sons in the village.

It won't be enough to do much more than supplement a pension.

It won't be enough to prevent the Dupont family from selling the crumbling family home to a Dutch family from Antwerp or to the American girl from St. Luis, or to the English photographer who documented the book

"Vanishing France "uniquely aware that he is part of the vanishing he photographs.

What else can they do but drive their 2CV citron vans, which look like rusty Australian water tanks on wheels to their tiny vineyards to cultivate with battered handheld rotary hoe, criss crossing the vineyards without wires, a knapsack to spray, the essential secateurs. This is viticulture little changed from the ancient ways of their forefathers, albeit the rotary hoe replaces the horse and plough. The two-horsepower citron replaces the one horsepower dray. The Gauloise remains the Gauloise, the blue jacket of the paysan remains ubiquitous, even if an Australian is helping the Dupont family, the old men know the Australians went to war with their fathers.

The second son of the Dupont family, Antoine is not like Claude. Antoine has no ambition or intention of working in the vineyard. He is leaving for Paris, as soon as he can, it can't be soon enough, Today is too far away. Antoine's attitude reflected in whatever he does with a practiced seventeen-year-old indifference he and Mathew hoe, trim and spread grey dust minerals under the vines. Antoine trying to teach Mathew a little French as they go. Mathew has no aptitude for language, his accent is woeful his memory is worse. Still, it is better than working alone and Mathew might learn something amongst his French jumble of gender, meaning, tense. He might manage to order a beer somewhere.

Antoine tells him stories, some of them true, some of them Franny says, you might not want to believe, of life in the village, the vineyards and the hills. Long strolls on the escarpment, with Antoine, Mathew and Megs, Antoine telling stories of our Socialist Mayor who has the privilege bestowed by law and tradition of being in charge of our voting rolls. A long queue of voters cast ballots for our Mayor even the dead Gaullists who changed their affiliations in purgatory and the others who have left us for Paris or Lyon would of course come back and vote for our Mayor if they could. Our Socialism extends to the way we make wine, the Cave Co-operative making an egalitarian wine.

Domonic with pleasure guided them through the Cave Co-operative explaining again but now they can see it, they should understand more how it is in the south.

"The Midi has potential which people just don't see." Dominic explains, "The South, they say, is one giant vineyard of ordinary fruit. It is not, never has been. I get to see it as they bring the fruit in, the best fruit I'm tasting comes from the vineyards grown on a strip of old escarpment just north of here extending beneath the ridgeline just before Saint-Guiraud. Not every vineyard is as good as the next, some of the old growers I think are too old, to do the things well, even if they knew how, which some of them don't. The very highest vineyards yield little fruit, and the lowest, in the valley, the flavors are dull, precisely the flavors for which the Midi is known."

"Imagine," Dominic added, "if we judged Bordeaux on the lake of poor wines they make each year." (A remark Georgia would repeatedly make.) Dominic pours them a glass from a long row of tanks, square concrete tanks either side of a narrow working strip, hoses and pumps awaiting next job, the tanks all abutting and thus forming a single green concrete wall, punctuated by stainless steel doors, racking valves, drainage valves and one sample cock, from which he extracts a tasting glass each.

Wine Tasting Notes; Saint-Guiraud, Tank 404. 1991.
Colour. Bright, vibrant, garnet.
Nose. Lifted fruit, confectionary, perfumed, cherry with blackberry undertones.
Palate. Medium weight, confectionary fruit follows into the palate, provincial herbs, savour, spice, chalky limestone tannin, hints of mountain meadows.

"This is the future of the Midi in a glass." Dominic exclaims.

It was Franny who found them the house with the blue door to rent from the American lady who lived in St. Luise. "The Americans came ten years ago, they have a love affair with everything French, but it's an affair, it doesn't translate to a marriage, they aren't very good at living in France."

The house has a blue door, blue shutters, but is built of stone like every other house in the village. It is universally described as the "blue house" as it is the only blue door in the village. The lady from St. Luise (if she had a name, which she obviously did although neither Mathew nor Megs ever knew it) had spent some time, some effort and good deal of Yanky dollars doing up the blue house. Decorated in Provincial style with just the odd nod to the

Hamptons according to Megs. Megs would know. Her one American indulgence a magnificent, expansive window on the upper story overlooking the village Montpeyroux and the distant river Herault. The window in the upstairs bedroom allows you to look out on the distant village church towers, Montpeyroux, St.Andre and beyond. The church towers chime the hour, one chime for each hour, twelve chimes for midday. The village chimes are not in synch. Each village has a different midday a few seconds apart. Montpeyroux begins, St.Saturnin comes in just before St. Andre and then Saint-Guiraud.

"Is that a round or a cannon?" asks Megs.

Four clocks, four times but only one priest who shuffles around to each church in its turn, delivering service to an identical congregation of elderly ladies, with rosary beads.

Megs and Mathew explored the villages, sometimes with Antoine, sometimes without. Exploring the countryside, sometimes up onto the escarpment and the much longer walk to the bridge on the Herault and the ancient town of Saint-Guilhem-le-Desert. A town wrapped in legend, according to Antoine, Franny just shrugged.

Megs drew the church of St. Saturnin, the church of Saint-Guilhem-le-Desert. She drew the vineyards, the old men on the bench, the same old men playing pétanque or on their two stroke mopeds driving out to the vineyards. Until she had drawn everything interesting in walking distance, at which point she became bored. A bored Megs is a difficult Megs, at least in Mathews eyes. A Megs who doesn't just hang around the vineyards, the villages of the Herault.

"We should go to Paris. Catch the train, stay for a week and have some fun."

This Mathew realized is not a suggestion.

"We should go to Barcelona."

This is even less of a suggestion.

"It is okay for you Matt (always okay for you) but I came here to travel. To see things. We should go to Barcelona."

They went to Montpellier. Franny drove them; to see the flea market and do lunch.

The French are very good a lunch. Australian's think lunch is a sandwich, the French think lunch is the "meaning of life."

"It will be fun, and we can buy Megs some paints, she should do more than draw." Fanny has been talking to Megs.

The *marche aux puses* underneath the aqueduct on the Boulevard des Arceaux. Junk stalls, stalls with nothing but postcards, stalls with photos and paintings and old clothes and walking sticks, the flotsam and jetsam of many, many lives. Franny loved the *marche aux puses,* this is a bibliotheque of stories awaiting my pen, awaiting my typewriter, awaiting the call of my imagination, a tattered wedding photo, a medal from the war. "Did our war hero die? Did the marriage flounder? Did the marriage soar? What about the walking stick, how does that fit in? Everything's a story, everything's a clue." Franny enthused.

Mathew didn't get it or didn't get it then, all these lives' written in junk.

Megs does. Megs caught Franny's enthusiasm and began to rummage through the stacks and stacks of post-cards looking for an image she can plunder, an image she can own. Many years later Mathew understood or Kato understood and helped Mathew realize there is always a larger story. In wine it is not just the names on the label but the stories of the men, and woman, toiling in paddock, cellar, shops. It is not just the length of fermentation but the person with the hose pumping juice across the caps of fermenting skins. Wine as an artifact of many people's dreams. Mathew hadn't yet contemplated those lives as they sat at the terrace table on the Place de la Comedie, only his and Megs.

This is Franny's treat, this is Franny's shout, therefore she gets to make the choice of wine and every course. "I want you to taste my south, you could choose so many wines but for me it is Gigondas."

Mathew had tried St.Saturnin, St. Andre and Montpeyroux, but Gigondas, changed everything, he began to understand, he'd tasted many, many wines, but none of them like this, wine which can unfurl sip by sip, a world, a tale, a place and time, this wine is a story in every sip. A great wine is similar to a great *marche aux puses*, it contains stories.

18.

Sete Harbour, Café Terrace (Late Spring of 1991)

Dominic's hometown: this is the place, this is the town, this is the harbour, this is the wharf. "And me," says Dominic, "a child upon the deck of the steam ship looking out at this "home "which it was not. It wasn't my home, my home was back in Africa."

A chaotic harbour, chaotic dismemberment, Dominic continues, "all I remember of the day is no one knowing what to do. We left the boat and here we stayed, one ferry ride from our true home in Africa. Next year Algers, as the exiles say, we are still here, obviously. They call us Pied-noir, African feet, my left foot African my right foot French. Let's sit on the terrace and look at the sea, sea and ships and comings."

Sete is not settled, it is anything but, it is a city of transits and each on the take. It's a flash harbour city, young men wearing gold chains, gold watches, meeting the African ferries with dubious help. Schemers meet dreamers on the dock of the bay, African touts, African marks.

"I can sell you a Rolex, assist you to stay."

Dominic ignored them, they are in his eyes, background noise, nothing more.

Dominic ordered the mussels, fresh from the sea, the Baston de Thais, just over there. Matched with a Frontignan, also just over there. Local wine, local produce, this is the French way, the true order of things. Megs with her sketch pad, drawing boats on the harbour with a squiggle of line. As much as she likes Dom, she knows once they pour the wine, the conversation will be wine and nothing else. The minisculia of harvest, crushing, fermenting, barrels or no barrels, blending and fining.

"If I were to make it, what would I do, what would be different, and what be the same?"

If Franny were here, Franny would entertain her with tales of Paul Valey, poet of the city, not quite with as much animation as she might if Paul Valey was her beloved Cavafy, the poet of Alexander. Or even Lawrence Durrel poet of the Mediterranean ("he is a neighbor you know, a fellow resident of our south.) Franny would have made sweeping gestures encompassing all ancient harbours; Marseille, Alexander, Napoli, Sete, and all the poets who hailed from them.

The wine, a pastel gold with a soft cornflower hue and the faintest scent of blossom. It is Megs appreciates an evocative wine, perfect with the mussels.

"It's good to drink a wine like this in the place where it belongs." Says Megs. On a golden day like this with her feet on second chair, looking out upon the sea, sketch pad balanced on one knee. In faded jeans and cotton shirt, floral greens, yellow, red. Wearing her battered travelling hat, stuffed in rucksack as we go, from London to Jerez, Jerez to Montpellier, Montpellier to Paris, battered, tattered but with a scarf wrapped loosely around the crown to give the old thing a lift, a burst of colour.

Mathew always says that she should include in her watercolour paintings a splash of vibrant colour, a bold and daring spinnaker, flying from her boats.

"Can you see one, I cannot, only one sail on these boats, which belong in Africa."

Old men from Africa; they meet them at the *Café Paix d'Afrique*, Dominic's father amongst the men dressed in their dashiki shirts, drinking the old wines they used to make and eating the spice tastes left behind. They speak a guttural French which Mathew cannot understand.

"History's flotsam," Dominic says, "He is my father, I understand, what has happened has destroyed the man. I, myself will not be them. I will not look back, I have future dreams."

Dominic telling Mathew of a possibility to buy land in La Rouquette. "An old vineyard left to die back into escarpment soil. A family long left to work in Lyon or Paris that is what happens in the south, it slowly, slowly empties out. We can have a picnic there. Come and see my southern dream."

"France is a picnic." Megs laughs at that. France is a picnic which consists of one bottle of local Vin de Pays, baguettes, crispy fresh, cheeses (plural) ripe Camembert, Rochefort, this is the south. Tomatoes from the market stalls they visited this morning, cucumbers, endives, red pepper and olives from the olive stall, salt dried, sun dried, with chilli, herbs, sausage, wild game terrine.

"France is a picnic", which must end, but not before Dom and Matt wander across the old vineyard. Kicking sods of loose baked red dirt, up and down the steepish hill. "Classic vineyard soil this, red clays upon a marl base, the terroir of southern France."

"France is a terroir picnic, Matt." Megs says, "We could eat this food in Australia, but it would not feel quite the same. Not the same as drawing the hills which Cezanne drew, in the colours he would have used. I don't know what terroir means but for me it means Cezanne, Van Gough, Gauguin, Dufy, everyone who has set up an easel in these hills where Dominic will plant his future."

One last dinner then Paris and Georgia

19.
Vanishing France, (The New York Times Book Co. 1975)

Franny's guest (besides Megs and Mathew), is the "famous" photographer of "Vanishing France." In the village of Saint-Guiraud, and in the eyes of Francois Bregis, the man a near celebrity. Harold Chapman dressed impeccably in a style which says British in the south of France, a blue blazer embroidered with presumably the school motto, linen slacks, pale skinned, lank, straw hair going grey. Harold had moved his camera lens from English fields to rural France. His lens, he says, is in command so he had no choice but follow. Thousands upon thousands of photographs, old men in the village squares, vineyard harvest, market days, shopkeepers, workers, everything.

"I didn't know what I know now, my France is slowly vanishing." Harold hesitates before he says, "Vanishing is not my word, I owe that to the editor."

Franny's husband Pierre retorts, "Perhaps it ought to vanish. Village gossip, village feuds, small, minded village attitudes."

"And yet, here we live, here we are." Says Franny, "Your counter argument."

Pierre and Franny niggling in Harold's disruptive presence. Franny liking Harold is not to Pierre's liking. Pierre appalled that Harold speaks only rudimentary French, "a man of images not of words." To Pierre's eternal disbelief and Franny's eternal amusement. This dinner conversation is entirely in English and not just for our Australian friends. And yet both know the truth of it, the young are leaving the villages, the young are voting with their feet. Even if Monsieur Le Maire does not think their votes went with them. They would have voted for him if they had come back to cast a vote. What of the village of Saint-Guiraud? What of the village of St. Saturnin? Dutch families buy the houses off the villagers to use over summer holidays. The houses are empty the French families have long moved out.

The Dutch families do not sit in village café, do not play pétanque in the afternoon, do not work out in the fields and do not buy the vineyards.

Mathew asks, "What will happen to the vineyards?"

Pierre suggests "The families left will buy them out. The vineyards of France will survive. We make the best wines in the world." End of argument.

Matt was not about to contradict him. Matt knows, through Dominic, it's not as simple as Pierre thinks. Dominic will buy one cheap, some will die a natural death, some ploughed in and some just left, and the villages will shrink. Mathew hopes it isn't true. Pierre is certain they will not, contradicting himself somewhat, "it's the genius of the French to find a way to modernize and still keep our traditions, not become Americans."

Nothing worse could befall a land, than to become American. A land of McDonalds, Hollywood, pop culture which isn't culture and "their wine, you know, they sell in jugs!"

Mathew would love to think that France could retain all of this, the southern vineyards, co-op wines, old men playing pétanque, but knows those old men will die, and too many young men have gone away. Some will come back home to spend twilight years in their village home, but never enough.

"The south," says Dominic, not Pierre, "Could learn to make a better wine, but the French genius to think the world should follow them not the other way is sure to make this messy."

20.

Georgia Best Parisienne.
(In the summer of 1990 one year prior to Megs arrival)

Georgia Best Parisienne; there is a piece of Parisienne graffiti, Dormir, Metro, travail , mort.(sleep, train, work, die) written on the wall of the Rue de Karl Marx Georgia Best thought at least they would work and die in Paris, it made all the difference in her eyes.

There are days which feel like that, not with the taste of bittersweet, rather there are days, just ordinary when Paris is a backdrop. It could be Melbourne, Paris End, (an old joke and not funny.) This is Paris Georgia tells herself and takes herself to a favourite places; the Jardin du Luxembourg (a cliché), Isle La Grande, Bois de Boulogne, Foret de Fountain blue, the Vignette at Montmartre. Boulevard de Georges Seurat Island of La Grande Jatte, another Paris cliché. A favourite painting of Megs who sees the world in colour. Megs would accuse Georgia of black and white and occasional forays into grey. Grey is the quicksand of a lawyers life and very hard to argue, "there is a right way Megs, however much you want to find, the interesting, the curious, the "I didn't know," the "who would have thought." What's the point of going there? Georgia thought there was too much grey indecision in both Megs and yes, Mathew however much she likes them both (and she does) They are so easily distracted from life's path.

Georgia Best is not.

Nearly always not. Georgia knowing that Megs is so easily distracted sent her a postcard to arouse Meg's curiosity. Send her on her way. On the back of a Seurat Postcard, the famous island scene, of course. Georgia wrote in startling red "texta:

Dear Stringer (Megs)
Have made it to Paris, As I always said I would. Found an Apartment when I'm settled you must visit, you will love the Museums here.
PS. went swimming on Surat beach, swam. into the painting, easy to find on the metro.
PSS. next the Gallic lover.

Sometimes Georgia remembers she lives in Paris just as she'd dreamt she would and other times she knows she lives in her shared apartment and travels to her office on the metro exactly as the graffiti testifies. There are the times when she forgets this is the city where Simone de Beauvoir used to sit debating existential angst. Georgia Best has never experienced existential angst much less debated it. Why carry such a toxic weight when there is so much more to do, so many boxes left to tick.

Paris, tick, I have made it here. I speak the language. I know the streets, have made some friends. More companions less than friends at least we always use the familiar "tu." Georgia Best also understood she lives in a world where friends can act as steppingstones to something far grander and where friendship can turn to rivalry, on a dime. Georgia played with the Yankee slang in Paris. It seems appropriate, there is much that's Yankee about Paris, Hemmingway and Fitzgerald left but their descendants linger in Montmartre, the Left Bank. "Disney Paris" Georgia called it, Montmartre even has a Disney toy funicular, ride up, ride down, she usually does. Mathew will tell her it is not a Funicular as with everything else in tourist France it only looks like a funicular.

21.
Dot McKensie, girl from SCEGS
(Sydney Church of England Girls Grammar School)

Dorothy McKensie (call me Dot) said to Georgia, "Careful, careful Georgia girl. It's a funny game we play, but Crikey girl a game it is, let's not pretend it is something else. Take it from an old hand like me, it can get quite messy."

Dot was not a Dot at all. She used the Dotty, class clown skit, well versed, well-practiced, but don't be fooled. Dot McKensie, a SCEGS Girl from the Western desert. "Back-O-Burke" she liked to say, bang it on when they are away from the Australian Embassy.

"All my life I have flipped between Jill-a-Roo and debutant, I am just as happy in horse shit as I am in Embassy bullshit, shit is shit. I do it well. A handsome man upon the arm, Italian, French or Englishman and yes in that order. There is a point, there always is, when you have to ask yourself, is this about to get out of hand? It has always been accepted Georgia that I will marry Russel from Goonabooka. I intend to do exactly that. I aren't leaving that life behind, however much I am tempted to. If I was from Sydney, maybe then, but I have country, as they say. We have country too you know."

Drinking beer, not wine tonight, shoot the moon in "country strine" tonight, "strine" is encrusted with outback grit, outback bull dust, outback insurrection. Georgia Best could not slip quite as easily between worlds. George felt self-conscious, in a Paris bar talking of outback country. Dot with a surer sense of self never left that life behind. He father's seat in Parliament, yes she would inherit that; honorable member for Grydir, it's her family fiefdom. Dot thought that funny, because it is true, funny true is funny. "You give a goat our family name and the goat would win that bloody seat."

Georgia Best did not reflect on anything that Dotty said, its piss and wind, just piss and wind, a Dotty talking frenzy. Beer in hand the outback girl takes centre stage, the diplomat out of sight and out of mind. Dot is not the girl whose motto is "good, better, best." The McKensie's aren't like that at all, the McKensie's, have connections. Dotty introduced her to Philippe de Courmartin, "have some fun (but nothing more)"

"The best and worst of France is Philippe." Dot explains to Georgia, "the famous arrogance of his class, a glimpse, a peep, a holiday in the world of Chateau France. Philippe's family are small players, no more than that but at least not *parvenu*. He can be fun and he's handsome, good wine, good food and the best of conversation. He can be generous, it's true, good for an adventure."

An Adventure but nothing too serious, "remember Georgia, remember well, don't let it ramble onto more."

22.
Paris Place St.Michel (Summer of 1991)

Megs has a Meg's list, a list of paintings she must see and which gallery they will visit to see them. Where the artist easel stood in her favourite Paris paintings. Megs says to Mathew, "I'd like to stand in the exact same spot. Buy a postcard of the painting, and you can take a snap of me on Seurat's River Seine, Renoir's café, Pissarro's famous Boulevard. I want to step inside each artists world."

"Overwhelming," Megs says to Matt as she walks through the Impressionist Museum, "I am walking through the best art book in the world and it's real. Matty, this is truly magnificent."

A joyous Megs, a wonderous, wonderful Megs, standing before a real Monet, a Degas, Pommard, Seurat. "We should step inside the scene, find out exactly where in Paris the artist stood."

"And buy a postcard of the each and every painting."

Megs has been buying postcards of Dufy, Cezanne, Gauguin. All the artists of her and Mathew's south of France. Megs has taken ownership of the escarpments, the red tiled roofs, cafes, village places, olive groves and cypress pines. The south is now and will forever be her France, the France of all her sketches.

They catch the metro to the scene of Seurat's painting on the riverbank but for all its amazement Paris is not Meg's South of France. Paris belongs to Georgia.

Georgia Best Parisienne, oh so chic, so self-assured. "So glad to see you Megsy girl. A familiar face in this crazy world."

Georgia says, "crazy world" in inverted commas to signify what a life she is having in this great city. The life she dreamt and now she has. The life she always described to Megs, "when I get to Paris Megs." The dream is now reality and "Yes" some moments are magical.

"So let me show you Paris Megs, the magic backdrop to my life."

A long walk along the Sienne to Pont Neuf and the Ill St.Louis, left bank art, Shakespeare and Co. Notre Dame. "So much life and light and Oh! So many lives before, artists, writers, performers. Of Course, we will spend tomorrow at the Musee d'Orsay."

"Yes," says Megs, "I'll go again, just us girls that will be fun. Mathew, needs to spend some time, applying for work when we get home."

Georgia says, "Baz is going to Indigo. Maybe Matt should try as well."

Indigo Wines, Northeast Victoria, Rutherglen region, it is an old family owned winery. Leske and Best once sold their wine.

23.
Indigo Winery, Chiltern. (Late Summer of 1992)

High Country, hill country, Megs says to Matt, "This could be our adventure in the land of the snow. The land of bush and mountain, new things to paint, this will be grand."

They rent an old Australian farmhouse just out of town near the river, not far from the hills with a view of Mount Buffalos northern slopes. The house is rambling and tired, it has the feel but not the space of Matt's Grandma's house overlooking the bay. It is conveniently close to the vineyards, close to the school where Megs will teach art.

Mathew had written to Indigo Wines from Paris France. Indigo Wines was number one on his list. Indigo was the "winery" to work at. Baz had told him so. Baz knew these things. Baz worked there.

Indigo Wines is a family company, one of the original family wineries. Gerald Jones the patriarch of the Family, the Senior Gerald (as distinct from his son, Gerald junior) took Mathew under his wing. He liked the lad, Mathew is keen to work, keen to learn and mostly keen to listen. Mathew will listen to an old man muse on an industry. An industry that old man has spent a lifetime working in. The senior Gerald Jones knew of Leske & Best, knew the family history attached to it. Leske & Best were Indigo's old wine merchants.

"This industry is close like that," Gerald explained to Mathew, "or used to be. It is changing now, the era of the family winery while it is not over, it is diminishing, the old families are selling out. It is becoming more corporate, the family winery simply doesn't have the recourses or the skills to compete. Personally, I hope we stay a family winery forever Matt, but I also want our industry to expand and prosper, to create opportunities for the likes of you."

Gerald and Mathew are bumping along the road in his old ute. They are going to Geralds vineyard. Gerald has planted his vineyard out with all the old varieties. "What will happen to them I ask? My old Ganache, my Tokay vines, and my Palominos. I feel an obligation Matt to produce those heritage wines. My son will continue making them or so he says but my son's son, that is a question mark."

They work in the old Grenache vineyard thinning shoots which crowd the centre of the vines and shade the fruit. Matty has a "eye" for shoot thinning, for vine structure. Matty has Ian "Hoppy" Stewart eyes. Matty can hear Hoppy saying, "don't cut that can't you see, if you cut there instead it cleans out the lot." Gerald was impressed.

24.
Vintage Indigo Wines, (Summer & Autumn of 1992)

Vintage, Indigo Wines, Mathew worked another Coq Continuous screw press (he must tell Dominic) and a Bucher barrel press for Indigo Wines. At least the Bucher press Dominic would mildly approve of. The Bucher press is not continuous. The Bucher presses one load at a time after which the press is cleaned and reloaded. The pressure can be controlled. The pressing is gentler. The Bucher press is in Mathew's eyes a much better press, if not state of the art. Mathew ran them both well, which means efficiently and quickly and while the press is a critical piece of infrastructure in the process of winemaking. The job pressman is considered so mind numbingly tedious that you can extract someone from the vineyard to work the presses over vintage. That someone is Mathew, vineyard staff know nothing about wine, that is well known.

Mathew is pleased to see Baz again, just to know someone at the new job would be enough but Baz is a friend. Baz works the tank farm, an enormous building containing all the stainless-steel tanks where the wines are settled, fermented and blended. Baz and Mathew must liaise continuously as either juice or wine from the presses will be pumped to the tank farm and Baz will need to have a tank ready for Mathew to pump into.

The grapes arrive at the winery from the home vineyard on tractors trailers attached, from the senior Geralds vineyard on an old Ford truck, and from distant warmer, irrigated vineyards on larger trucks. Always in large two-ton bins which will be emptied into the crusher hopper to be crushed and pumped across to Mathew. The white wine grapes pumped directly to the press while the red grapes will be pumped to the overhead fermenters. Crusher to press, press to tank farm.

The crusher is Campbell John's domain. Officially the whole process, crusher to tank farm is Campbell John's domain, from coordinating the trucks, the crushing schedule, therefore the press sequence and onto the tank farm. The two crucial variables being to always begin with white varieties and finish with red varieties to minimize cleaning and to have somewhere to crush the grapes into either an overhead fermenter, or an empty tank in the tank farm.

Campbell John is a lean man, very thin, very tall, and gawky. Campbell Jones is always referred to at Indigo Wines as "Mr. Green Acres" as Campbell could not pronounce the words; Grenache, which he called "Green Acres", Gewurztraminer, which he called "Gee Wiz Traminer" Mathew and Baz loved that one and Muscat Gordo, which he called "Gordio". Campbell Jones was a peculiar man, not just his mispronunciations, he has a twitching energy, a nervous, jumpy, back and forth, duck and weave energy, at what, who knows? Campell John co-ordinates the fruit arrival, the trucks coming and going. Machine picked fruit in the cool of night arriving early morning, handpicked local fruit arriving in afternoon and evening. The trucks with machine picked fruit will need be processed quickly allowing them time to turn around and be back in Swan Hill, Shepperton or Mildura in time for the night picking. The crusher crew as well as Mathew and Baz must begin work very early in the morning before the trucks arrive and process the trucks quickly once they have arrived. If at all possible they will try to process whites before reds to save clean down time. It is Campbell John's job to co-ordinate this vintage waltz; the trucks, the crusher, press and tanks.

Campbell Jones is the second son of one of the old families. He didn't really want to be his brother's forever junior. So he set out on his own and works for Indigo Wines while he builds his own vineyard and winery. He is really not the junior type. He was the captain of the local football team, Captain of cricket team, Captain of the Crusher.

"A good captain sets the bar for his men. He leads with actions not with words."

"It's just as well." Matt says to Baz," since he can't pronounce them."

In spite of his peculiarities or maybe because of them both Mathew and Baz had enormous respect for Campbell John and the impossible job of coordinating vintage because things go awry, often. And when they went awry Campbell John would rush between the crusher, press, and back again, and back and forth and back and forth. Campbell John's run is more a charge than a run, a staccato, jerking forward, a tumbling bantam rooster flap between crusher and press, checking, checking. Checking Matty knows they are following the "Gordie" up with "Riesling" following Riesling up with reds. "You need fermenter seven ready," which Matty knew he had his work sheets. John would return to supervise the change from Gordio to Riesling which they did with nothing more than a bubble of messy air. Pumping air through the wine hoses is the quickest way they know to change varieties. It is also the worst way to change varieties, water would be better. An air bubble is not good for pumps, nor for separation of Gordio and Riesling. There is always some mixing which is not that important when you are crushing a semi-trailer load of fruit but very important if you are crushing a precious half ton of Chardonnay from a new boutique grower.

"A little Gordo in Riesling Blah! when your doing twenty tons "Not so Blah, Blah, Blah when they began to do half a ton of precious fruit from a first time grower.

The image Matt will always keep of John is one of frozen in indecision. Spied from atop the high gantry John is stuck halfway between the Crusher and press. He jerks a foot towards the press, reverses towards the crusher, back and forth and back again a rocking doll which oscillates a jelly quiver on concrete strip. To which disaster should he attend to, the disaster Matt is about to cause or the equal disaster about to descend on the crusher crew?

There were disasters none of which were ever solved by John's panicked oscillations.

The day the bottom floor fell off the overhead fermenter and twenty-five tons of Shiraz poured out a tsunami of skins and fruit.

The night the crusher power box exploded in a New Years Eve of sparkler bursts and acrid smoke.

The evening after many hours of tipping bins the pins just snapped, the bin and two tons of grenache and bin chased into the hopper crusher screw mangling everything.

Minor disasters you expect; the day a bicycle in two-ton bin jammed up the crushes screw. The occasional overflow of juice because Matty forgets to check his tank. The day Matty forgot to attach his suction line to press tray because he had drunk after a long lunch on Easter Sunday.

John was never frantic then, he'd shrug, smile and say sometimes these things happen in vintage. Worse things happen at sea (He'd never been to sea).

And then there were the other times. Baz and Matt on the gantry, just a little time to chat about the process, what's coming in, where is it going, which fermenters empty, and which tank "Are there any?"

"Crickey Baz!"

"There will be in an hour."

"Make it half an hour or I'll pump the juice onto your floor."

Not a lot of time for chat, catch up on Matt's trip to France, but enough. Time for Mathew to tell Baz about the year in the south of France. The Cote Du Rhone, Cinsault, Mourvèdre and Grenache. (Or Green Acres as they call it here.) Baz should plant some Green Acres in Navarre on the land Baz's grandfather has allotted him.

Mathew mused, "It must have reminded someone once of the place in Spain, similar climate, similar feel, similar hills surrounding."

Great Western country, shale rises, sedimentary flats. "I have gentle East facing hills, not as warm as North or West which I suspect is an advantage.

The talk in this era is "cool climate wines," ill-defined, but plainly not Baz's block in Navarre.

"I can't afford to go down South." Baz will explain, "It is the land I have, family land. It has good shale soils. A little like the soils of Great Western from which we know can make good wine and so can I. I will plant the obvious, Shiraz, same as Great Western but not so sure of the white wine, perhaps Riesling."

Matt suggests Frontignan, Muscat a Petit Gains Blanc the wine of Sete.

"Perhaps" he says.

"And Grenache, blended with Shiraz, Mataro, or Cinsaut."

A conversation, they would return to, again and again. Grenache the perfect grape to grow in the town with Spanish name. The grape of Navarre. Navarre Victoria yet on the edge of a lessor, so much lessor Pyrenees Range.

"But what of you?" Baz asks Mathew.

Mathew didn't know. He certainly no plans to grow grapes or any land to do it on.

The second statement is true, Mathew had no land, the first is not or not completely true. Mathew has no plans at all. Mathew has ill-defined dreams but dreams aren't plans, they are something less. They don't take root in shaky ground. They can move and change and morph but never become a reality without a push and shove. The bigger truth is Mathew isn't ready. Mathew doesn't know enough.

Mathew had convinced himself. Dominic and Baz knew more, even Campbell John knows more.

And then vintage was over and they held the traditional post vintage BBQ. Tasting the first of Vintage wines early Rieslings from the Riverland, early Shiraz and very early Pinot Meunier. The Riesling is a simple wine, simple and unfinished.

"It has fruit and little else, but partly that's our process. " Baz summarizes, confident he can do better. Baz Lehman, the farmers son believes in a small scale winey where you do everything yourself. "You can play around, experiment in the vineyard, try different things. Not be bound by the imperatives of production. What if you picked some fruit while it had more acid and has softer fruit flavours? What if you picked the shaded side of wine before you pick the sunny side? I want to try out these ideas and more. You can't try things like that in a big commercial vineyard."

Mathew had never thought it was possible to "play around".

"At Agricultural College," Mathew said, "we are trained to grow our fruit, with attention to the cost, disease free and ripe but never once was it ever said, we should begin to make the wine out there in the paddock."

"Why not?"

Why not? Mathew would have to think. Mathew would carry that thought back with him. Back to the vineyard, next week, next year and for many more, an unresolved nagging thought. We can make wines out here as well, in the vineyard, in the closed wet air, in the crackling frost on fidget wood, blue winter sky's and piercing air.

25.

Mickey and the Kid (Winter of 1992)

There were set positions in the vineyard ute. It is how it is done or how Mathew preferred it done. Mathew drove, Mickey sat in the middle, and the Coonawarra Kid took the far side seat. The rest of the casuals, old pensioners mostly sat in the tray. No one said it was fair. The Coonawarra Kid graduated to the cabin because he was the most amusing, not the best of reasons, but the reason nevertheless. Mather's natural bent is not the privilege of the cabin, but someone must drive or else they'd stay in the vineyard car park.

Smoko is always on the tray, all for one and one for all, "Hoppy" Socialism prevails.

The Coonawarra Kid is not from Coonawarra nor is he a kid. Coonawarra is older than Mathew who is older than Micky although not as old as the tray folk, old pensioners by and large, earning a little on the side. Coonawarra has the build, (self-described) of a German tuba player parading on a National Day through the streets of Bavaria dressed in lederhosen, naturally. "Splendidly rotund," Coonawarra says. Coonawarra fills the front seat amply and while he plays the tuba it is not his instrument of choice. The Coonawarra Kid was once a student of the; Musikschule der Stadt Wein, Mathew had him say it thrice, it has an air, a harmony. The Coonawarra Kid would not speak German to either Mathew or to Mikey.

"Why should I?" he says most seriously. "Language is a way of communicating and I cannot communicate in German with you guys who don't speak German. Do you want me speak Tibetan". (They considered that a joke, it wasn't.)

As was his name on Mathew's part.

Mickey had asked, "who is that guy?"

"New vineyard manager from the Coonawarra." (Both untrue but both stuck)

Coonawarra was a man of gigantic enthusiasms, coupled with some real talent and a photographic memory. His enthusiasms, came and went, snap your fingers something new, something new was wine this year. Coonawarra owned a property in the hills, the soil and climate of Burgundy. Coonawarra should know for once he played a piano recital in Dijon, France. (Mozart Piano Concerto No.17 in G major K 453) If he remembers correctly and he does, Coonawarra has an eidetic memory. Neither Mathew nor Mickey would ever doubt him in case he told them the page number he was quoting from. Coonawarra had been to Montpellier knows the folks down in the south but the south, is not, he pronounced, where the future of wine will lie. Coonawarra's opinions boomed across the vineyard as he told stories of his traveler's tales.

Matt with village stories of Saint-Guiraud, the harbourside of Sete. Pruning appropriately Mataro. Last to burst and first to prune, chardonnay pruned last since it will burst first into risk of frost. High country air, high country snow up in the mountains all around. Three times a year, sometimes four, blizzards rage across the hills, dusting lower slopes with white, as low as Coonawarra's vineyard. On the upper slopes it lies white and gleaming in the last autumnal days of vintage you can see it from the upper gantry. As you can from the old farmhouse and from the vineyard but only while fresh snow lingers on the snow gums of Mount Buffalo. Mount Buffalo being neither as high nor as snow covered as the main range.

Talk, talk, talk, which became a game to while away the pruning hours keeping pace on each other's rows, a game invented by Coonawarra mostly who knew many curious things and had or at least appeared to have an encyclopedic knowledge. A trivia game, name a river with every letter in the alphabet, name a mountain, a capital city. "I will name a region in France, you tell me the allowable varieties. Mathew begin with Bordeaux, excluding Entre-deux-Mers?"

"Cabernet, Malbec, Cabernet Franc, Petit Verdo, Semillon, Sauvignon Blanc."

"Mickey, what did he miss?"

Mickey shugs.

"Muscat a Petit Grains Blanc. We are pruning it although it is misnamed Tokay. It's not enough the name is wrong," booms Coonawarra, "Tokay is a Hungarian town which produces a "Tokay" wine, and not from

Muscat a Petit Grains, but from Furmint. Am I pruning Furmint now?"

Mathew doesn't think so, although it's obvious to him, there are at least three varieties, maybe four, all ancient gnarly vines but with very different growth patterns.

"They grew Muscat a Petit Grains on the coast around Sete, we drank a bottle on the harbour with my friend Dom." Mathew reminisces.

Mathew began again talk of pastis, pétanque and stone walled towns, old men in the village squares and their ridiculous Citron vans; full of vineyard hoes and rakes, secateurs and knapsack sprays. To reminisce about cake, coffee and Cote du Rhone. (Which the wine he is referring to isn't.) It is a V.D.Q.S. Vin Delimite Qualite Superieure, made from the same grapes, grown in similar country but not Cote du Rhone, Coonawarra point this out sabotaging Mathew's monologue. Coonawarra had been to Tokay what he played there he doesn't say what he played since he now knows they are by and large ignorant of good music. He does say he went there during the Soviet times. "Which proved to me that socialism is not a friend of wine, wine you see is feudal."

Coonawarra has drunk muscat on Samos, in Frontignac and Piemonte. The Piedmonte wine he considers the very worst, drab and sweet. He will be planting Pinot noir in a climate parallel with Beaune or Pommard. Coonawarra has had a Stevenson Screen installed and all the instrumentation to finally settle the dispute which "cool climate region" his vineyard belongs in. Cool enough for snow to fall, lingering days after biggest snow dumps.

"It is" Coonawarra explains, "important to gather facts not the sort of wished for maybe, nearly, almost, well in my opinion. I have a climate like Bordeaux which folks round here will tell you they have on the sole basis that they want to plant Cabernet. Where I ask you is the Gironde, the maritime influences from the coast. People always make things up, call a block Tokay when it's many, many things but Tokay isn't one of them. Call a wine Burgundy when it's made from Syrah, only a few hundred kilometres wrong. What would they say if I played a minuet in G in F sharp, because, well because I liked F sharp best, which I don't, by the way."

26.

Black Range, Brown Deck, Red Ploughed Paddock

Coonawarra's shed; a "Lysaght's" steel farm shed, lined internally with cheap pine slats, pot-belly stove raging, one corner partitioned as a bedroom. The shed facing east has solar panels and a battery pack, circa 1988, cumbersome and bulky. Coonawarra's put the system together following directions from a Popular Mechanics magazine. They are off the grid. His wife Lisa a Californian girl is lanky and accented but not loudly so. They met in a Buddhist monastery in Ladakh. Surprisingly, he did not make that up.

On Coonawarra's shed deck, looking north in the subdued mid-winter sun Matt, Megs and Mickey are lazing about. Megs complete with sketch pad, drawing Lisa. "An interesting face," Megs comments, "Not classic, but with character."

Megs asking Lisa about the snow which Coonawarra has told Matt falls sometimes upon their land.

Lisa doesn't like snow. She answers, "for me it is not a novelty. I come from Northern California, not a southern beach girl not the California of sea and sun. Northern California can be freezing believe me. And in Ladakh the winter was bleak. John (which is Coonawarra's real name) used to ski of course, in Austria, when he studied there."

Megs with feet upon a stool sketch pad resting on her thighs is doodling, "Just doodling" she says to Lisa. "It's nothing more than that," Lisa sitting half-lotus legged, a grey shroud wrapped around herself. The air is cold, the sun is warm where it strikes upon you, otherwise the afternoon is bracing.

John (Coonawarra but John at home), Mathew and Mickey discussing sunlight, warmth, and temperature. The microclimates of the hills, pockets of warmth and pockets of cold, how the air slides off the peaks.

"It's called the catabolic effect," John would know, of course he would, he has read, everything. He can tell you the page numbers and from which book he is referring. They no longer even ask.

"It's not consistent," John is trying to fathom the mystery of air. "Air and frost and mist all flow off the high peaks following contours of the land. I ride a B.M.W. motorbike which is the perfect instrument to investigate the flow of cool, or the islands of heat. You feel it as you ride around, especially in the late evening every pocket of cold and heat the warmth which radiates from the rocky ground and the rivulets of freezing air. When I turn into my drive I can feel the subtle warmth, more so since I ploughed my ground. So while I am cooler, being high I am also warmer than the surrounding country, a perfect micro-climate. You can feel it warming us as we sit in midday sun."

Talk slid into France as Coonawarra John explained the correlations between his land and his beloved Beaune. The continental climate with its large temperature ranges, the cool moist summers and long cold winters. The hours of sunlight over the year and the heat retaining properties of his northern slope.

"I think I am probably south of Beaune, perhaps closer to Haut Santenay. Anyway, I will let you know once my weather station starts gathering data."

The Department of Meteorology had supplied it. They said they had very few stations throughout the hills. Their only demand of John Coonawarra was to report each and every day to them or at least have someone else to do it for him. It takes a season for one result and one season can be deceptive: unusually warm, unusually cold, or very, very normal.

Coonawarra John prunes at Indigo that year and he will prune the next one.

27.
Summer heat. (Lake Catani Shores)

In summer heat another shore, a place to escape the heat below, sweltering in the valley, in the vineyards. John Coonawarra's weather station pinged a high that sweltering summer February, just too high, for a gentle Cote du Beaune. Megs and Mathew depart early morn to drive the mountain road which twists and turns to the Mount Buffalo Chalet and the lake below it. To sit, to swim in the not quite ice melt lake, or lie in the cool snow gum shade. Mathew hesitant at the water's edge, he never will just jump right in. Tea brown water, grey green trees, with magnificent ghost white snow gum trunks carved and gnarly, twist about, battered by the blizzards.

The air is gelati, lemon mist, the water "bloody freezing." There is a photo of the lake hanging on the wall of the Chalet. The lake in winter with ice skaters gliding upon the then frozen lake.

"I'd love to do that," Megs exclaims, "I'd love to skate in a winter fairyland, come up to Lake Catani and see it in the snow. We should come up don't you think?"

It's not a question. It never is, it's a statement. "We will do this Matt." Quietly dressed up as wish. Mathew recognizes a wish like this drives their relationship to do something, something different, something new.

"We could go with friends from school. They are colleagues Matt." Megs says, "It's a big distinction."

There is a shyness about Megs, in Merbien she had Francesca, who had Rod, a little cluster of first year outs teachers this school is not as welcoming, this school has friendships long entrenched, and Megs has struggled to break in too any established cluster. She doesn't have what most she needs, one friend to paint with out in the hills. At least some colleagues have asked them up, to introduce them to the snow. "You must see it. You must come." These are the mountains which they love.

"And you will too, Mount Buffalo if you like, but it hasn't had good snow for years, It's too low, and rarely has the good cover it used to have."

"I've seen photos of skaters there, on a frozen Lake Catani."

It seems that was a different age.

Meanwhile Coonawarra rants, "it doesn't make sense. It can't be true. The temperatures I am getting from my weather station contradict all the historic records. One year's data is not enough, it could be a misdirection. Any warmer and I will be pushed, far, far south of Burgundy. The old records I don't think would have gotten this so wrong. I mean it's only one degree, one degree wrong it ain't much, but it adds and adds and adds, if you want to duplicate Romanee Conti which is my dream."

Not so perplexing if you are Baz, up on the gantry during vintage time, "We have been farming our land in Navarre since before my grandfather's time have seen things change and change again. It's getting drier Matt and I suspect it's getting warmer, not so much if you ask my Dad, let's say it's complicated."

Another vintage, endless hours, Matt is more efficient now, knows exactly what to do, just as well for Clive does not, new guy on the crusher. Campbell John flaps about, hither thither, "Oh my God! What a circus! What a scene!"

In the chill night towards the end of vintage under arc light, high above the press and crusher, on the gantry Baz approach with a sample bottle of the wine they're making. An old Tokay, except says Baz, "This is a sample from the old barrels. This sample an original, one hundred years it has been down there, refreshed of course but all the same the closest thing to drinking with the ghost of your great grandpa."

"It's the nectar of the Gods," says Baz, and Baz this time ain't lying.

"I need a sample, can you get me one, need show Megs and my mate John."

And then it's done and dusted.

28.
Winter Snow Mount Buffalo Peaks (Winter of 1993)

Hugh McCarthy and his wife Jess are exactly as described by exuberant Megs, bushy, bearded folk who know all the Latin names for flora and fauna which grow and slither about the snow covered tracks. A gentle drizzle turns to snow during the final twists and turns up towards the chalet. At the chalet ski hire putting on the hire skis is an awkward experience. It's a slippy, slidey thing, not so much for Hugh and Jess, who happily give instructions. Actually, too many instructions and somewhat contradictory. They would be better off with less, just the bare essentials. How to stay upright, according to Megs, staying upright would have been the most useful instruction. The snow is mushy, the snow is wet, the snow is cold when you spend too much time upon your bum. Mushy snow is good to learn; mushy snow is slow and soft, colder snow is hard and fast, it's also dryer, but neither Hugh nor Jess mention that. It looks so easy, just glide along, it looks like something they should be able to do. Following Hugh and Jess, out along the snow gum trail. The mist is now a mist of snow, swirling in the still, still air falling ever slowly. Winter snow scene, white, white mist, white snow, shadows of grey trees within, dripping snow melt off the trees, falling inside winter coat. The scrape of skis across the snow following the tracks of Hugh.

"Bend your knees," Jess yells at them.

"They are."

"They're not, you are too upright. The more you bend the less you fall, and you are closer to the snow."

Megs bends her knees, even more, as they begin a slow descent. They tumble, tumble, as their skis decide to race them down the hill. Another lesson halfway down courtesy of Jess. How to turn and how to slow. Just enough, enough no more, to get them safely around the track. It's a short loop out and back, with a perfect place to rest, upon some granite boulders, looking out into a lifting landscape mist.

In a landscape of grey, grey white, a silent landscape, blanketed, a landscape meditation.

"Thermos" coffee, Jess's fruit cake. "Take your skis off walk about," In the slushy, mushy white, knee deep in drift snow, "It's why we ski."

Hugh is telling Mathew how the alpine flora survives and even thrives in this cline. They talk about the temperatures, the wind and wind chill, it seems the alpine country is, Hugh, is certain, Matt less so the canary in the climate shifts,

"It's getting warmer on the peaks, the snowfall not so certain, not reliable, we don't ski Mount Buffalo any more we go higher now to the main range above Falls Creek." Hugh explains.

Megs is sketching a world of white and faint lines of something else, granite boulder, snow gum trunk, frame and edge the world of white.

Back is not so difficult; back is not quite on their bums. "At least says Meg, I've done it now, I understand the beauty."

29.
Dijon France versus Muscat a Petit Grains

Snow is blanketing the hills, above the deck in Coonawarra John's shed where Coonawarra, Mathew and Mickey are discussing weather stations. John Coonawarra is in a spin, "It's the numbers, they are out of whack, I adjusted for my height from the historic figures from the weather station at King River dam. The river dam weather station may be cooled by the presence of the lake behind or the temperature has changed or perhaps this year has been a particularly warmish year or I have placed my station in just the wrong spot on my land. Every month my readings have placed my vineyard further south further down the river Rhone I'm now in bloody Cote Hermitage, Australian Burgundy, here we go."

"How do we know we can trust the figures out of Dijon, France?"

John Coonawarra simply gave Mathew his most withering look.

"It simply isn't funny Matt, this is my dream, my vision. I could pretend I didn't know, just use the figures from the dam, but I am, if you haven't noticed, a little bit pedantic." Coonawarra John understates.

Mather grinned a lopsided grin and says, "If it gets much hotter, you could grow something like this," and pours a glass of the old Tokay Baz had pilfered from the cellar. Thus in the cold mist shrouded day in the middle of July upon the deck of John's old shed, wrapped in coats and scarfs, Mickey in his beany striped annoying black and white, Matty in skiing balaclava they share a rare glass of wine made from the Indigo vineyard in its youth, from a mystic faraway time when Great Grandfather Lieske sold this wine.

In the deep mist chill of winter hills, in the morning of the day the warmth of perfection meets John Coonawarra's soul. "Jesus bloody Christ!" he says. It is hardly a description. "Where the hell did they bury this?"

"Down in the old cellar."

"I don't mean literally, this wine a revelation. I am trying to make one great wine, a Romanee Conti on my land and all the time one of the worlds great wines is lost in the cellar of Indigo Wine. Bugger!"

Snap, it snapped, loud and clear the snap of Coonawarra's complete attention, he began reading, compiling information.

A list which began with the words; Muscat a petit grains. And the wines;

Stetubar.

Rivesaltes

Beaumes de Venice

Constancia

And as this passion arose it began to eclipse his hope to grow the next Romamee Conti on his land.

"You dream of growing a great wine and here is one and it's ignored stuck in an old cellar, lost, forgotten while Indigo Wines makes nothing short of commercial crap."

Coonawarra Kid, began to doubt his attachment to his land and the wine he would make. The great clouds of Coonawarra began to tremble and grow. Darker and darker and suddenly a bolt of lightning, "an epiphany sirs." No longer the man who will grow in the hills, the next Romanee Conte, his mind has moved on as minds can do, and John Coonawarra's mind does violently.

Mathew did not even come close to predicting what a fluxed Coonawarra Kid actually did. Mickey may have.

John Coonawarra brought a rucksack and said, "you see this farm, this house, this life it is the top of a funnel lads. You see this rucksack, it's the base, everything is going to fit into this rucksack or my bank account."

He's heading off, he is on the move, California first but then France to join a Buddhist commune.

"There is more to life than wine and much more than ambition. "Om-namme-padhe-hai", John said it thrice and vanished

Which was surprising by itself what happened next floored Mathew to the muddy ground. Mickey went and followed. "He'll be back, the world will eat that naive kid up."

Even stranger is it didn't.

Mickey and Coonawarra Kid's Wine; Muscat a Petit Grains.

Origin; the origins of the muscat family is obscure, as it has been grown since early antiquity, having a long history in Egypt and Persia. One suggestion is that the muscat family originated in the country of Oman, in the city of Muscat. While the Greeks will claim it hails from the Greek city of Moschato.

Muscat a Petit Grains.

Muscat with the small berries, Muscat with the large berries, although there are many would probably be the closely related Muscat of Alexandria. Both Muscat a petit grains and Muscat of Alexandria are used in the production of fortified muscat wines; the French vin doux naturel as well as Australian Liqueur Muscats.

Also known as; Muscat blanc, Muscat Frontignan, Muscat Lunel, Moscatel, Muscat de Grano Menudo.

The variety is notorious for colour mutations and can be found with shades of colour from white through to red and deep brown/black.

Famous Muscat wines include; from France, Muscat de Beaume de Venice, Muscat de Minervois, Muscat de Frontignan, Muscat de Riversaltes, the sweet muscats of Greece, the famous desert wine of Constanta, South Africia, and the muscats of Rutherglen.

Flavour, Muscat a Petit Grains has a floral, grapey, musky aroma, as well as citrus, rose and peach notes.

Interlude No.3;
Wine Evening, the kids, Goa Café (Present minus 18 months)

(This is not a date!)

Two-Stroke invited Madison. Madison invited Onna. Onna invited Jake. Two-Stroke hoping to woe Madison. Madison wanted Onna as a foil. Onna not wanting to be the third wheel of a Two-Stroke tricycle invited Jake who was about the boat shed picking up saw-dust compost. Jake who likes her.

"He is keen on you," or so says Reggie.

Jake with mini-Malibu strapped to banged up Holden ute, he wears an Akubra on his head. Jake hasn't shaved and hasn't showered other than in the ocean. Jake has salt crusted hair, shabby shorts, elastic sided Rosso boots with elastic floundering, the shirt is newish embroidered with the logo of his business. A generous smile which is good even if it includes an edge of the awkwardness of the boy inside, which may also be good.

"This is the place," Two-Stroke says, "for the best fish stew I know of Portuguese mixed with India. Hybrid vigor same as me otherwise known as a mongrel dog, take a fish stew spice it up, and don't forget the coconut."

Two-Stroke loved being first to know first to find, first to taste. Rev that motor, let it rip leave the others in Two-Stroke dust. He found Goldie Reason, "How's the label going Maddy?"

"It's fun," says Maddy, "the girls a scream. She decided years ago, not to be bound by unwritten rules and skate about the written ones. She wants her labels to say one thing, this is me, love me, hate me. I don't care, or maybe just a little bit, but not enough to turn away from my true direction. Her labels must align with her, fearlessness in all she does."

Two-Stroke loves the grand design, make a statement, take a stand.

Two-Stroke's mouth begins to rev, carburetor overdrive, "I love my history, love Matt's lost wines but don't you think we are creatures of the future." And instantly contradicts himself, with a description of the soup, a soup of exploration. Caravels around the Cape of Good Hope bringing Portugal to Kochi shores, Saffron becomes Turmeric. "Studies in yellow is what I think, as I am," Two-Stroke adds with a jackal grin.

Is it "yellow" Maddy ponders, it's more a jaundice tan, perhaps.

"I'm half Irish, half Japanese," Two-Stroke explains again they suppose this time for Jake, "how that even happens is in and of itself a mystery, but what a vibrant yellow. Colour matched with the wine a Vinho Verde, it's not "green" however much the name implies, more the colour of unripe lime."

Onna shuts-up always does when the talk is colour, not because her mother paints, no the reason's simple, she sees colours where they aren't in the grain and feel of wood, in the textures of her life. No one needs to know, about that shit, thank you Dad, don't mention it.

"I choose the wine" so Two-Stroke said, "to reflect the Portuguese." But Madison cannot help but think they should have drunk a Manzanilla instead. Vinho Verde will never prompt a postcard on the postcard wall.

Onna quietly watching them, Madison and Two-Stroke. "They aren't a couple", Maddie's said, but they have a couple kind of dialogue made up of gestures, nods, and silences between. Onna's has her father's what? Naivety, incomprehension of the simple currency of love, she cannot see from where she sits across the table watching this, that they are not a couple. Even if Madison had always said she wants a man who gets the very essence of herself which is her art. It is who she is. Two-Stoke doesn't get it.

"I am the girl who does her art, it is me and I am it. I'm not sure Two-Stroke can or will ever understand. Oh! he gets that I can make, amazing labels which he can sell. (Do you think that is an Asian thing?)"

Onna is confounded by the animation between the two. What is true and what's a fib, fibs are maps where all is wrong, where landmarks are and are not there. Onna cannot navigate in a world which moves about. Wood is solid, joins more so, a join can't fib and be a join nor rivet be a rivet. But this observes Maddy is a two-way street. Maddy doesn't want to ignore the boy who sits with Onna. Is this a "thing" or just a friend? The nearly handsome surfy boy with the swimmer's body makes some noise, has things to say not as much as Two-Stroke, but then who does. Not about the wine, he is a boutique beer lad at least he's not someone minus a sense of taste. He would love to go one day to Portugal not just to surf the Nazaire break but to Sintra gardens.

"They have an easy sort of feel", Maddy keeps observing, "it is a lot slower than you and me, but Onna's like that. She has her dad's laconic style". Maddy says to Two-Stroke, in summary of their night at the Goa restaurant Eastern Beach.

Ships upon the harbour, rusted tramps on oily sea, awaiting landing Eastern Wharf. Plastic checkered tablecloths, assorted unmatching knives and forks, plates and cup and everything. The waiter is from Portugal, Goa, out of Melaka, who Two-Stroke met the other day selling wines for Bay View Wines. "I stock wines from Portugal, but please visit my little café, bring your wife or girlfriend."

Bored with Vinho Verde, and torn between a late picked port or it's modern variation. Maddy had an inspired wish. "I cannot see it on the list but do you have a Setubal, we have never tried one."

Jose Baptista had never once been asked about that ancient wine. A wine, a style, lost to time, no one even knows this wine excepting Jose Baptista. Beyond surprised, he says to the four young folk who shouldn't know his Setubal. "Wait a moment." And returns with a bottle and quickly pours five glasses for he'll join his surprising guests.

"It is a muscat although not as sweet as its Australian counterpart nor as dense if that's the word, but this is how I like it. Less liquor and much more wine you can drink it with the soup. Try it, try it! If I may interrupt your dinner."

Jose sat upon a chair between Madison and Jake. Jose is more Kato's age than theirs deeply brown, a craggy face, more Indian than Portuguese, "They have a word a sense, a song, let me introduce to you "Fabo", the sweet nostalgic longing of the Portuguese. Setubal is Fabo in a bottle."

"When Goa returned to India, (we always say that with a spit of phlegm), we did not ask for this return and where do we return to? We were Goans not Portuguese my great great grandfather jumped ship there and yet, and yet in Portugal I am too Indian both in skin colour and attitude. Who knows my family left for Melaka out of some nostalgic hope we could never be Malay so we left again. This time for Australia. I tell my story to guests who ask to try a glass of Stetubar I've told it once, that is today, the only price you have to pay share my story, share my wine."

"A deals a deal," Two-Stroke says, who knew something about not quite this and not quite that.

"We dropped our suitcases on Station pier where no one else has deeper roots and everybody feels the same foreignness. We are too white, we are too brown, forget our history start again, welcome to Australia. Australian's only really know Goa for its beaches but never for what happened there, it's long embroidered history, fortunately they like to eat, like to drink, perhaps with a nostalgia, for a holiday in either land, Portugal or Goa but never once have I been asked about my Setubal or told about my Fabo. Wine, you see, it must be balanced in itself and balanced with a story for wine is a story in itself " (Much as Kato always says it is).

30.

Jules Dupont Again (1st. person singular)

You will all now appreciate they all have their fictions which they believe of themselves. I have no doubt their made-up worlds delightful. Our Madison, great artist in waiting, she has at least some talent to give credence to the dream. Two-Stroke with whom I synthesize, I can shift from Aussi/French without a blink, with a mere twitch. He cannot. His Asianness imprinted on his face. Even when he doesn't want or when the world don't want that face. Even if the world is only one Madison Golightly. While Mathew wishes that he was born with the handsome face of his ancestors. Great Grandfather Leske a striking man in the dark intense nature of his clan. D.N.A. can be a bitch when it contradicts our narrative. My mother is not and never was a contradiction to herself. The Scottish Western District Squattocracy have kept it in the family. She had to go and marry out, to a Frenchman of all things who married out himself of course to produce some hybrid vigour, me!

My vigour's intellectual. I am not deceived by what they say. The stories which they constantly tell each other and themselves which is why I am your translator in this what? They are my friends. I recognize, they are faulted, fractured, pushed in many ways that contradict themselves.

The science of wine I understand the science of friends is baffling.

The Postcard from the Aube was written in green ink

What, a wedding,
One of us,
Since when have we been old enough

The postcard was sent to Megs from Georgia, knowing Megs was enchanted
by the South. Enchanted, such a French word.

31.

George Seurat on the Riverbank (Spring of 1995)

France is different the second time around less new and more familiar,
less holiday more wedding. Georgia Best is getting wed in Bordeaux and
Megs a bridesmaid at least one person form the school. "So why not
extend a few months this side a few months that, visit Mickey in the
south. What the heck, we deserve it Matt."

      Domaine de la Motte on the Midi channel bank an Australian
vineyard in Midi France what a contradiction. Even more so that young
Mickey should be the one to manage it.

Young Mickey the lad in camouflage greens Indigo Wines vineyard apprentice, studying viticulture. He graduated two years ago and set out on an adventure. Mathew cynically believed the adventure would be short and shallow. Naive Mickey the country lad would be eaten up by the big bad world. Matt was so very wrong and genuinely surprised to be so.

Mickey roamed far and wee found work in London in a Fine Wine store. Worked a vintage in Champagne and visited relatives in Sicily. Mickey met a entrepreneur while selling fine wine in London, an Australian with the vision to start a winery in Midi France. Scotty Davidson had a dream, a scheme, to make French wine with an Australian feel for the Australian market. French wine with Australian feet, Australian's farourite varieties with an Australian winemaker flying in. Its why Domaine de la Motte was so familiar; the trellis, vines, machinery. This wasn't Saint-Guiraud. There are no stone walls, no bush grenache, no 2CV's or old village men in the square playing pétanque. This is international wine, this is the future. No village Cave Co-operative for Domaine de La Motte, modern wine for modern times. The old French ways are vanishing, the old men are too old now and no one will replace them, no sons or daughters for why would they spend a lifetime on this soil.

Narbonne on the channel bank Matt watching Meg bent over her drawing pad sketching channel traffic. At the lock house, sketching the old lock man in his blue French overalls directing boating tourists. The impatient *Anglais* ignorant of the French ways and of lock procedures. The English tourists hire their boat in Narbonne Quay arrive at the first lock, this is the first lock - no excuse - where on earth did they expect to be two hours later, Bezier, Montpellier? Megs sits upon the channel bank with her paints and a makeshift easel dabbling in water colour, a smudge of blue a hint of green. enliven up the channel bank, a quite animation.

Mathew contemplating the many tastes of Midi France, doodles in his notebook. The metal taste of lock and boat, a muddy damp, a jumbled air, places taste like what they are wines don't always correspond. No one ever said they should. "Megs can't paint the things I taste." It's never been that easy. Paint our way through Midi France. In search of Muscat 'a Petit Grains to complement and to compare with Indigo Wines Old Tokay.

Searching slowly through Coonawarra's list;

Muscat de Frontignan

Muscat de Mireval

Muscat de Rivesaltes

Muscat a Beaumes de Venise.

This is an ancient Greek and Roman land. There is a roman ruin on the hill which overlooks the vineyard. Mathew and Megs sitting on a roman wall, Megs painting sunflowers in the fields. Megs in floral straw hat dress, sandals bathers underneath after an afternoon at the river Aube.

In the late, late afternoon, no need to hurry back today, no need for anything at all.

Quiet days in Languedoc.

Mathew in the vineyard helps out Mickey "on the black, but whose to care only those in Paris Blah!!." Mathew's has left Indigo Wines. He took the opportunity to go, "back to France with Mikey there and Coonawarra should be there." Coonawarra isn't. Where the hell is he then?" Mickey doesn't even know. "He left an old Ford Prefect car, left hand drive with English plates not the best car to drive around it is so obviously English." Yet the perfect car because it's there parked in Mickey's garage. Scoot about in local roads over to the river Aude swimming at the weir beach grassy bank and amble shade refreshing beer in weir cafe, naturally its France, of course there is a little bar. The water chill in river flow out of distant Pyrenees.

Megs still damp from weir dive sketches in the light she wanted most. Megs belongs in summer warmth in summer heat under summer sun damp and wet from the sparkly brine, if not from muddy reservoir. Mathew found a Muscat de Minerva at the wine merchant from Cuxac d' Aude which they share on grassy bank. Megs is contemplating not the wine but in her head a scene which George Seurat might paint not exactly Matt in Akubra hat, but riverbank and folk at play lunching on the grassy bank, swimming in the weir.

Georges Seurat, Bathers on the Riverbank a favourite painting of Megs although it wasn't Midi France. On the Seine not the same clear southern light. Paris light is softer. "Impressionist beach" Megs has seen the painting in the Musee d' Orsay. Stood on the exact same place from which Seurat painted it; Rue de Mouffetard near the Place de la Contrescarpe on the Seine. Megs had a vision on the riverbank watching children, families Megs is musing on Georgia marrying. "The time is ripe, the time has come, Megs has decided then and there. Matty need not know right now. There is a time for telling Matty things, not yet, not now, possibly not tomorrow.

Megs sees a daughter a new "Chilton girl", a daughter in their life, she paints this unborn daughter onto the riverbank, imagining every detail of a life they might return to. A house on the hill with a glimpse of the sea for Mathew's delight. (He should move back to his old grandma's house which is neither for sale nor in their budget of zilch when they return broke, again.) Flat broke, unemployed, and pregnant, to boot. *"Tant pis"* as the French would say with a shrug and a smirk, "she'll be right." and she knows it will. Megs knows, she just knows, she has faith in their lives things will turn out. Megs has faith in the colour, faith in the line. Faith in life that she's painting filling in holes the light and the shade, the shadows, benign beneath the trees in the sun. A vision not yet seen completely neither it's colour, nor in its detail. Meg's preferred water colour because it hasn't the focus. Blue sky she can see the dappled shade which has the distinctly scattered eucalypt shade the grass of summer not so green and somewhere above the screech of cockatoo, breaking the air.

32.

Cultural Differences Aside

Phillippe de Courmartin sparkly new and shiny when he drove Georgia down to Midi France to visit her Australians. "Planting a vineyard in Narbonne, extraordinary but *tant pis*, Narbonne is not Bordeaux, it barely counts as France at all."

And so began a long discourse on the subtleties of France. In Phillippe de Courmartin's opinion, Languedoc is barely France at all, nor it seems is Corsica a land of bandits, Roussillon a land of Catalonian smugglers. Phillippe de Courmartin, a handsome man in a very Gaelic way, swept back hair and darkish tan, brown eyes, the nose of Charles de Gaulle (he is a Gaullist after all). He sports a fine moustache the pilot type but no he is not a pilot. Philippe dresses well, if conservatively, he is from wealth, a family chateau in Bordeaux (where else?) apartment off Rue Haussmann (again, where else?) A man whose politics whose car (Citron CX) whose clothes speak of, if not another age, at least an age whose time is spent. Curiously Georgia has said the same of Matty.

Georgia Best is "best." Georgia deserves this kind of man. Georgia was destined if she'd stayed home to marry a Western District equivalent of Phillippe de Courmartin. Georgia Best told herself, this is better, this is right speeding through this sway of France with her so French lover.

Cultural differences aside she waves away what niggling doubts under the vast cover of the word love but then, just then, the differences were the spice between them.

The charming Phillippe brought his chateau wine to display his generosity and educate these Australians, who it is known are inhabitants of a savage land. They are therefore ignorant of all things refined. Mickey speaks French, albeit, with southern coarse inflections. Mathew's French nothing more than a mangle of disjointed words, Megs the schoolgirl version. They will speak in English even though their English is not much better.

Mathew who calls himself a winemaker and a vigneron embarrasses himself today. Mathew doesn't understand Bordeaux wines. Mathew's palate is lost in Australian fruit cordials, sunny wines lacking in finesse, with no structure and certainly no history. Mathew described Phillippe's Chateau wines as, "slightly dusty on the nose which extends into the palate, subdued stew fruits, plum with brassica overtones." Phillippe turned to Georgia in French and asks if he's an idiot.

"We have grown grapes in Bordeaux when Australia was no more than a savage lands, well that is wrong, Australai still is. If this is what they think of wine, proper wine, not cordial."

Georgia Best embarrassed by both Mathew and by Phillippe tried to explain it all away, "New World – Old world, different styles", leading the discussion away from Phillippe's under-appreciated Lessor Cru Bordeaux towards a larger question. Is there an Australian style? An Australian take on old world wines? Do we have to forever ask are they the benchmark for Australian wines?

Georgia asks, "Is Bordeaux the benchmark for all Cabernets around the world and if so which Bordeaux? There are many, many Bordeaux wines not all of which deserve the appellation."

Georgia defended Phillippe that day and would defend him again, and again with less and less conviction. Phillippe de Courmartin's cellar does smell ever slightly (and sometimes more) of the mold and damp and dust. It smells of old barrels, ancient casks, an ever-present waft of what, mushroom, truffle, forest floor and his wines smelt of the cellar. Now that Mathew points it out Georgia cannot ignore it.

"I sincerely hope I am wrong'" Megs says privately to Matt," but I'm not sure if Georgia will be content with Philippe with his Bordeaux life, on his terms, so far away from the farm girl, the Chilton girl, the Georgia we know best."

Philippe understood the why the Australians gravitated to the south into the sun, the simpler wines, simpler tastes, simpler lives of Midi France. Why they are interested in those southern curiosities, the muscats of Frontgnac and Sete, Minerve and Riversaltes. Phillippe can help Mathew and he will, his family knows family, an introduction, one phone call. Surprising Mathew with this generosity and that his blaise attitude to one phone call. "It's nothing."

He rang a family in Frontignac. "I have some Australians in search of Muscat a Petit Grains, every variation."

His family knew their family.

"In France," he says with intonation suggesting there is no other way, "Connection counts, it is the way, it is simply how we do things here."

"Are you sure you are an Australian?" Philippe says in French to Georgia who ponders are you insulting me or them, Georgia could not decide just then at that moment she wasn't sure which side of the insult she would like to be with them or him, not for the first time nor the last Georgia is caught in a dilemma?

"During my French years," she'd one day say, "the year I lost my bearings." (North by north west, bearing south, Mathew at the wheelhouse.)

Mathew's direction to go and find Dominic in Saint-Guiraud. To do so he will need to use the dreaded French telephone. The French telephone he knows will be answered in French. And while he understands a bit not so much by telephone. The woman who answered understood, the name Dominic if nothing else.

"Howdy mate!" says Dominic in his best Australian greeting, "when you guys coming up."

"On the weekend, leaving Friday morning."

"You won't recognize it," Dominic said about the place, all the changes he has wrought.

Actually, it's not much changed, except in his eyes it is transformed. The vines are flourishing that's true with a newfound vigour. Dead vines replaced judiciously, the worst of vineyard gaps, new vines planted where dead vines were.

"Reluctantly but necessarily," Dominic explains, "there is a quality to old vines, I do not want to dilute too much. Yet a freshness to the new, you see the dilemma an ancient one. Balance it always is a little good a little bad, everything a two-edged sword. The south is like Australia Matt it needs that lick of sweet fresh fruit. Let me show you the cellar Matt, I've made some changes, Ive..." he says. But said no more until he opened up the giant wooded cellar door.

What was once a dirt floor barn, old barrels, older casks, museum vintage crusher, press, which is the only thing he has kept.

"As a pressman I thought you would appreciate my old press. You clean them up and they work a treat perfectly adequate to make my reds."

"Note" Dom says, "the tile floor, the new drain points, brand new stainless steel tanks did away with wooden casks (fifty years of caked in mould) the old barrels (just as bad). New barrels in a barrel stack on the back wall which has been sealed with waterproof render halfway up. The sandstone wall above it and above that a battery of lights installed.

"If you can't see you can't clean."

Such a Dominic thing to say. In the late, late night at Merbien Wines Mathew turned off the main lights to do a fast clean and get some sleep. "Just hose it down don't see the crap we will be back in what six hours. No one will see it before we do." The logic is inescapable.

Domonic, "blew a fuse," to use the colloquial, "We never, ever do that Matt. We don't do shortcuts, there is a discipline to making wine. It doesn't matter what's the time. How late it is, how long we have been here, eighteen hours. I don't care. Everything we do, we do the best that we know how. It isn't hard to make good wine if you do no more than that. Nothing is that hard in this job in and of itself. I mean there are hundreds of things which we must know, hundreds of processes we must do, just do each and every one to the best that you can do, starting in the vineyard."

"Clean the inside, clean the out, the underneath and inside out." That was Dominic's great creed, his mantra and his secret. Dominic believed in clean, clean fruit he would pick out the worst of fruit before the pickers would arrive. Clean flours, thus the tiling, clean tanks, (and clean valves it's important Matt) clean water to wash down and clean air (no one ever thinks of those.) Dominic had constructed an elaborate paper cylinder half a metre in diameter which snaked across the ceiling and attached to a two way fan drawing out the stale air and drawing in fresh, crisp, predawn air.

Dominic's mantra, number two, "I don't want to taste your winery, tired wood or packed earth floor, old mould walls or smelly drains. At Saint-Guiraud I did my best at Chateaux Narboni I'll do the rest."

Tasting; Chateaux Narboni, Vin de Pays, Grenache

Juicy, dense fruit, fruit pastille, confectionary, clean, nothing but fruit, with the slightest, subtle scaffolding of wood (Central France oak) lingering chalky tannin.

In honour of Megs he has a picnic lunch, France is a picnic after all. The same picnic, the same place, where she painted his vineyard beneath the Cezanne escarpment.

"I still have that painting Megs."

A table spread with tomato, endive, cucumber grown, from his garden, local bread and local meats, and local pickles for we live simply here in southern France. "That suits my Mr. Time Warp man," drinking Muscat a Petit Grains brought up from the town of Frontgnac.

"But tell me Mathew about Narbonne Australian's making wine in France for the Australian market. Australian trellising, Australian varieties the ones they know, Chardonnay and Shiraz. Global wines for global times. Personally, I prefer my wines to be an expression of their land, their dirt, their tiny patch of country. Vin De Pays I am proud to make, all wine is Vin de Pays if you strip away the pretentious appellation. It comes from country, speaks to it. Embrace you country wines my friend."

The Postcard from Sete was found in the Poche de Merchant.

DOMAINE de St-MARTIN-D'AGEL - E. GRANAUD, Proprietaire - Les Vendanges

Poem (in French) by Paul Valey

"The wine lost.... The waves drunk!
I saw extraordinary figures
Leaping across the bitter air..."

33

Sete sans Dominic (Late Spring of 1995)

The town of Paul Valery (Poet), port of Languedoc full of hustlers everyone is on the take, everyone has a "stick" more than one if truth be known. A town whose appellations crime. Meg's and Matty know it well, Dominic once had taken them to eat muscles on the quay to see the house of Paul Valery first time in France so long ago. The first and "Yes" the grandest. The First adventure of their life, the first and "Yes" the fondest.

A slightly older Megs and Matt eat fresh oysters on the Quay drinking Muscat de Frontignan (the vineyards just beyond their sight).

"We should go back to the sea again." (the lonely sea and the sky) Megs wasn't quoting, not least this time, rather talking of their future. "You love the sea; you should go back to the sea again."

A glass of Muscat de Frontignan, lighter than expected, "It has a kind of wispiness, an etherealness, a whiff of muscat perfumed by sea or perhaps the opposite, sea salt perfumed by muscat, and a sensation of sweetness as if you are biting into a slightly tart berry."

Sete, on the terrace, overlooking the harbour, Muscat de Frontignan drunk with Huitres de Bouzigues, local oysters, Sete harbour splashed in sun fishing boats riding moorings, ripple waves, the slightest breeze. Megs beneath her travel hat slightly bent and battered from being stuffed in her backpack, flung about. She looks relaxed, restored, resolved. Mathew thinks she shouldn't yet be talking of home when they have not completed his muscat quest. Yet even as she plans ahead, she is looking at the play of colour across the sea the blues, the greens, distant pale horizon. Smudged by clouds over the coast of Africa. Mathew knows a plan is forming in her head and not without surprising twists, she is thinking of going back to teach at Chilton Grammar of all things.

"I know I have said some awful things about the school, but not the art department, Lithograph presses, pottery wheels, kilns and space, light and air and the worst students in that school are the likes of a younger me."

Some things unsaid, some things are not yet formulated, or best left out particularly the daughter who Megs will send to the school on a teacher's discount. Even though she is not conceived, not yet, but not for lack of planning. In the absence of another plan, a plan by Mathew would never come up with Meg's plans are always the default decision.

"What of Mathew?" Megs asks Megs, but doesn't yet ask Mathew a few vineyards planted there, a few and very, very small, hobby vineyards, can't justify employing Mathew's until they grow. Mathew can do other things. He can turn his hand to something else she is more confident in Mathew than Mathew is in himself, but today there are other plans Muscat de Frontignan.

Another lost wine, another wine which once was sold by the old firm on Collins Street. The old ghost would be proud of them if pride is something ghosts can feel or maybe he would have just a wryest smile, enigmatic, incomplete. Megs could paint the smile except that she is not a portrait painter. Landscape with figure, singular, small and unobtrusive in Australia not so hard, a landscape devoid of people, in France people everywhere it is the first thing that she noticed.

Winery visit as arranged by Phillippe de Courmartin, Muscat de Frontignan. The building is grand French gothic grandeur in façade opulence of another time, southern French with oche stone, terracotta tile, blue wood shutters either side of palatial windows. A tasting is conducted in a room of Versailles elegance, a room of many paintings of grand mirrors and a high chandelier ceiling. A tasting for just Megs and Mather with Pierre winemaker for the Chateaux.

The Chateau makes four wines, they will try them all.

An unfortified Frontignan; "we are making lighter wines, wines we think have a modern feel for the café simple "Yes" and pleasant "Yes?" The taste of muscat driving it with just a touch of sweetness. I think the Italians can do this well the right balance between the fruit and residual sweetness. It proves to me that muscat is a very versatile grape, of course this wine is not allowed to use our appellation. Even here in the south where rules are less than Paris".

Just as Phillippe emphasized!

The sweet wines, *Vin Doux*; we make three, the most traditional matured in oak with a candied sweetness, honey, orange marmalade, summer fruit and citrus peel, peach and apricot, pale white flowers. A lighter version which is picked less ripe more like a Spanish Fino. This wine tastes of sea bleached by sunlight crusted in a salt spray and raw seaweed. "I find this wine," Pierre says, "matches perfectly our *Fruit de mer*, have you tried our local mussels on the quayside it's traditional. I also make my middle wine, less candied sweetness, less density, but more weight that my lightest wine as a middle son I think the middle can be overlooked. My middle wine looks towards the hillsides the *montagne*, a wine for poultry, wine for cheese, those foods beloved by the French. Whereas our traditional Fronticnan is luscious, sweet dense candied fruit not quite as rich as the Australian style which I know and love to drink."

"Come, I'll show you into the heart of our cellar, the fruit arrives, it is pressed outside, fermented in our concrete tanks."

An alleyway of thirteen tanks either side, you wouldn't know, two continuous walls of white, the tanks are square, each abuts the next, the only distinction is thirteen stainless steel doors with racking valves. The tanks are four metres tall with two gantries running over the tank tops just underneath the massive oak beams. The room has a cathedral feel with its oak beams and massive oak doors either end through which they enter and leave. To enter the barrel room itself, even more massive. Seven oak casks line one wall which are more wooden tanks than barrels. The casks have a wooden door for cleaning inside, for scraping tartrate off the walls. Mathew knows he has done it. There is a hierarchy of what goes where. The best wine to the barrels (Allier) stacked two high along the floor, resting on big beams of oak.

"The traditional Frontignan wine goes to barrel at least for a year but some wine sees more. Whereas the simpler style remains in concrete tanks we don't want that wine to see oak, oak would destroy it's freshness."

All of which was logical exactly how Matt would make that wine. Blend some wine from barrels with wine from cask to make the middle wine. "We also leave some wine in tank, some fortified to give the blend just a touch of freshness."

Pierre then did an un-French thing he asked Mathew about the wines he had helped make in Australia. Pierre knew enough to know their wines where at least the equal of their own.

"I want to ask about the skins, something we have been playing with traditionally we leave our wine on skins for one day before we press. I think we should try to play with skins. It is not the French way I know for sure we don't like to try, something different, something new."

Pierre and Matt taste variations on the theme from various barrels in the racks, the casks and concrete tanks. Variations of time on skins, the traditional overnight, two days, more days,

"Let us state the obvious, time on skins is not just that, time on skins is time on pips and petioles and bits of stem, and each and every one of these, has influence upon the wine. What do you think," Pierre asks.

Matt prefers the wine left on skins just enough to take on a tinge of colour, just a tinge. "It adds dimension to the fruit, an extra layer if you like, maybe "weights" a better word. It is a more substantial wine while not crossing over to rose. But I admit my prejudice is with the muscats I am familiar with, it's always hard to break with that to see a wine with clarity for itself and nothing else, however much we need to."

"I actually prefer the same" agrees Pierre, "and for the reasons you have said. It's not a wine which we can make for the colour unacceptable. Some falls out but some remains but what I've found if I use this wine in my blends the colour disappears but happily the flavour stays, in the background just beneath a sort of flavour underworld. I come from Sete, we have a reputation keep a look out for the sting, the twist, the unexpected. I give you Sete within a wine to drink upon the quayside. Would you find that in Bordeaux?"

Mathew knew they never would, especially in a Phillippe wine, but they are about to go and see.

34.
The Low Pyrenees Limoux

Skirting north of the Pyrenees, (in the car the Coonawarra Kid had left) through a very different south, mountain Cathar fortress ruins, river beech and native pine, terracotta brown turns green, brown, green. They stop in Limoux for some wine; "Blanquette de Limoux Methode Ancestrale (ancient method) a perfect wine for the Midi Pyrenees, made from local Mouzac grape, A sort of grape made "scrumpy", unfiltered, undisgorged, a taste of green apple and green grass. It smells exactly as the riverbank where they picnic, stop to sketch. Slightly cloudy, slightly sweet both the wine and day and place and perhaps this time with Megs. Scattered cloud or scattered sun, one way or the other, Mathew lying on the ground sipping wine and taking notes, contemplating Method Ancestrale in this land of heretics, Cathar, Huguenot and Vichy Franc, it has often found itself on the losing side of history. A land of ruins where history is told in secret or never ever spoken of. There are always secrets. There is always untold stuff, not exactly or not exactly not. The murky world of the imprecise.

Matt watches Megs sketching oaks a singular look of focus. Who is this person and what are they, he wonders, does it matter if grammars right? This great mystery, you and me, and why are we together? She chose me, on that distant briny day, out upon the pier. Splash we splashed into it all, boyfriend, girlfriend, and then more.

Travelling, travelling," just you and me babe", as they say, travelling asks us questions; so much time together, so much reliance and differing needs to sketch or drive even now Matt impatient to press on there is no need to hurry. There is no time they have to be anywhere except Bordeaux and not for days. Lie of the grass write some notes on the taste of scrumpy wine, haphazard notes at best. They have learnt a little about the room, the space to give each other. Megs painting space just like now, for her this space is breath, is air, is her voice, her soul, her soar.

Mathew doesn't like to say but sometimes he resents it, such a stupid thing to say, to think it even more so.

Travelling this time is easier; France is not so foreign now they have a little language just enough to get by, to order food, to ask for wine, to find a room and ask about where is this and where is that? And understand the answer. It isn't much but it's not naught.

Mathew always thinks that Megs will know the whatever it is he doesn't. Megs is the solid ground he walks upon. She is the reason they are here. She will be the reason they'll go back, to live in by the seaside.

She of many, many plans one of which is taking shape, plans within plans so long as they are moving on, moving forward to somewhere.

Meg's sketches do far more to capture the essence of this place, its air, the gravel vineyards, the native pine, the olive trees than Mathew's notes ever could. The egg-shell grey, grey-brown, grey green of granite escarpment, an ancient and deeply weathered volcano. Mathew can taste the fragrance of the pine in the wine, the herbs in the valleys and vineyards. Meg's watercolors fill the void of written word. transport you to that place and time take you to that bank of stream.

"Share a glass no other way to experience this wine, which will always be even diminished by being transported from its native land, both wine and poetry cannot be translated from their terroir. I love the taste of Gigondas because it always takes me back to that restaurant in Montpellior with Franny, but I think Megs," sighs Mathew, "your paintings do it better."

35
High Pyrenees Caurterets (Late Mountain Spring 1995)

It's an echo or perhaps an echo of an echo. The spirit of the old Leske's is here, Alexander Leske was a devotee of old spa towns. The Leske family owned the spa water from Buffalo springs not the worst of their old schemes. Mathew driving mountain roads, a *deja vu* of a peculiar kind, he doesn't pretend to understand. I've been here before it makes no sense, no sense at all, an epigenetic memory.

Megs explains upon a mountain trail her father, (a most peculiar man) liked to dabble in the unexplained; a butterfly in the amazon, flaps its wings and what is this a snowstorm brews in the Pyrenees. Megs neither believes in nor doesn't believer in the spooky stuff. Her father's archaic machines cannot measure all the ghostly things and what they can't measure don't exist according to him. There is a mystery deep inside, (a lull, a stop, an interlude, perhaps a misdirection) Megs accepts what her father cannot.

Why listen to the ghostly stuff expect the ghosts inside ourselves who are always there and always will be parley to your inner faults, inner doubts and inner indecisions. Ghosts be dammed the air is clear, the mountain side luxurious.

"A Chablis air."

"Summer meadows crocus flower, flora del sol (a lovely name) iris, moss, and alpine tuff, native pine and juniper. A picquet air thin this high, a ghost of green, mixed with grey brown tumbles scree, beneath the pines yet in the sun they spread their picnic groundsheet. The air is Chablis but Matt drinks the ancient Limoux bathed in dull green shade of pine.

Megs is painting mountain sides.

"I'm seeing silver, no chrome I think, I can taste it in the air, when I paint it and only then, it is more sensation than a taste, your stupid sense dyslexia has spread, it's quite alarming."

"Let's not exaggerate," he says, "sometimes smell and taste and sight, slip and slide between themselves, scent can be a memory, flooding us with images, childhood images when we did not differentiate between our senses, all was new, a kaleidoscope of senses."

Megs is the colour of rose champagne with the slightest hint of bronze, wrapped in a red one piece, bathing suit. Especially in her happy mood. Megs is happy now, in the softness of stubble heath, in the pot-pourri of flower, pine, in her summer floral dress, in the slowly ebbing warmth of high mountains peaks in sun, valley's in the shadow, in the last moments of the day. Megs takes his hand, envelops him in sweat and wine and prosaic things, she tastes of pine and turpentine, but there are mysteries beyond sweat and breath, sweet passion, sweeter consequence, on the fields of southern France, in exquisite mountain air, on crocus bed, and twilight mauve, both the colour and taste of cloves. Meg's conceives their Thursday child, under the tutelage of Matty's ghost, no more than a tone of greyish white and a voice inside his head a signpost to his destiny, that is a half joke nothing more, Mathew has no destiny.

Georgia's Wine; Semillon

Semillon; a golden skinned white grape which produces the famous sweet wines of Sauternes, Barsac and Cadillac, and dry white wines of the Hunter River New South Wales. It is a native of the Bordeaux region and was once the most widely planted variety in that region, now famous for it's red wines.

Cultivation; Semillon is a consistent producer, it ripens early but its large bunches are very prone to rot, thus it's association with botrytis wines.

France; Semillon is mostly grown in the Bordeaux region where it is blended with Sauvignon blanc and Muscadelle. It can be found as a dry white wine from the appellations of Pessac-Leognan, Graves, and Entre-Deau-Mers or in the sweet wines of Sauternes, Barsac, and Cadillac. (Note all three of these appellations are either in or abut Graves.) In Australia it is found in the Hunter Region. Once known as "Hunter River Riesling" in an era when Shiraz was misnamed "Burgundy" and Colombard "Clare Riesling". It can produce a wine of great complexity and longevity. Exhibiting intriguing honey, honey suckle flavours with citrus, lime and green apple, a aged Hunter River Semillon having a characteristic "lanolin" flavour. It is at it's best from the cooler years and when grown on leaner gravelly soils.

Interlude No. 4; Harbour Side Sydney (Present minus 18 Months)

South Coast oysters, north coast wine, Hunter River semillon, Georgia has invested in this winery. Occasionally she goes North to help with harvest as a cellar rat. They tolerate her, a shareholder who has made wine in Bordeaux. The winery is not a good investment. The lawyer inside Georgia Best tells the winemaker inside Georgia Best. The winemaker doesn't listen. The winemaker just want to play with grapes and juice and marc and wine. Winemaker Georgia wants to prune and press her beloved semillon. She mostly wants to sit and gloat, this is my wine, "I helped make the bloody wine!" to Dotty, meeting up today.

Georgia Best sips her wine the pale straw a reflection of her hair not quite as magnificent as it was framed with flowers on her wedding day. She and Dotty comparing notes, comparing choices, comparing dreams. Those fulfilled and those which are not. The dreams they once gas-bagged about in a Paris café.

Dotty has done what Dotty said she would do, she has ticked each box.

"It was a good path Georgie girl but not without its compromise. I took my dad's seat in parliament as I said I would, local member Western Plains. Married Russel as I said. He is exactly who I thought. Think of Earn your good old Dad solid but you understand. A local member spends a lot of time on the road which suits me, suits my marriage."

"Look at us," Dotty laughs, "In Paris we played Aussie girls, in Sydney playing Parisians, sipping wine and talking crap. Let the Vaucluse ladies stare at my R.M.Williams boots, I went to school with those dam girls, know them too well to be stared down."

Too many country miles have carved maturity into her handsome face. This is who I am, she says, always does and always has. In the embassy Dotty was a little bit off-putting.

Occasionally Dotty makes her think disturbing thoughts about herself. If she'd lived as Dotty does? Best is only really best reflected in someone else's eyes. Georgia is the best people say; lawyer, analyst, mother no. What would Georgia think or do if "good, better, best" was defined only by her and not what people said and thought. Who would she be behind that door? The girl who Earn would like her be dagging western district sheep, couple of sturdy farming brats. No Juliet, no Espie girl. We make our choices *"tant Pis"* she says returning to neglected French.

Change the subject something fun she tells Dot about old Mathew's game of wine. "Send a postcard from a town, a wine you love, you champion. One which belongs on Mathew's wall, the great lost wines. I must admit I'm the best at it as I travel more than those small-town guys."

"How is your Mathew?"

"He is not mine."

"He is and always has been."

It is an old tease Dotty likes to watch her blush and brush away the fact that Mathew is slightly more than she is willing to admit to herself, if no one else.

Mathew's post cards, "Let me see, what would I post if Dotty where in the postcard crowd? Not the obvious not for me. "Vin de Paille" a Jura wine, once again an old straw a little corner of forgotten France which I love about it."

The postcard from Bordeaux was written in cursive scroll

MONTRÉ & Cie, Négociants-Propriétaires a Bordeaux
EYSINES près Bordeaux ·· Une vue de nos Chais

River right and river left
In between is somewhere else
Someplace that it happened.
The postcard was written by George and sent to Megs.

36
"I do" It is Traditional. (Late Spring of 1995)

Chateau Haut Rivage is and always was on the wrong bank of the river. The north bank of the Gironde near the town of Cadillac. The south bank of the river Gironde is the ancient heart of Bordeaux wine, Sauternes, Barsac, Chateau Haut Brion. Phillippe's family prides itself on its truly ancient roots; they have tended their vineyards near the town of Cadillac since the fifteenth century. The chateau is an old farmhouse with a grand façade, two turret towers, five large windows looking out onto a Versailles Garden. The chateau with an air of long neglect no longer the source of du Courmartin wealth rather the opposite, Georgia suspects. Phillippe prefers to spend his time in his apartment than in the drafty shell of ancient family seat. Georgia Best is adamant, "You promised me a Chateau."

"I am a country girl at heart, a country girl needs country things." For her that is the cellar, barrel room, the vineyard rows which tumble down to the flowing river. (She married him for the vines, divorced him for the cellar. She should have known, she had been told but didn't listen, could not be told.) A marriage arranged that very year a "Grand Affair" for their "grand affair" it should have stayed and nothing more. A Chateau wedding this summer and everyone invited.

Megs and Dotty to be her bridesmaids.

"We are going Matt, it will be fun, back to France you will love that."

It's all planned out meticulously as only Megs can plan it, the trip to France, to see Micky and Georgia and some travel in between a chance to paint French countryside.

In Aquitaine, not Australie, "We do not marry in shearing sheds." Which Madame Dupont understood to be a sort of barn, the kind you might see in the Auvergne, or heaven knows in the Jura.

Madame de Courmartin (Madelaine) Georgia calls "La Countess" a title she would love to have is inevitably dressed immaculately in shirt and blouse, coiffured hair and fine make-up. She even known to wear gloves regally as a Countess should. (Georgia used to wear those things at school, now only in the vineyard) Phillippe's father habitually dressed in a banker's suit. He is charm personified, silver hair, a handsome man, carrying just a little weight. He defers to the La Countess in all things home.

"The wedding is not just for you", Madelaine explains to Georgia. "I'm sorry if you thought it was, it's a chance for family, to put on its plumes before the world. The cellar, you say, you'd like to wed, in the cellar, a peasant girl, would do that, why we have a ballroom."

It's a "Ballroom" in her mind what it is, a large sunroom once upon a time it was a pleasant room where beaus could meet chaperoned by spinster aunts that it is no longer so is a tragedy and more a tragedy is that La Countess will not see it. Georgia, from a *"pays savage"* speaks a passable French at least and her family once, La Countess was told, owned a famous vineyard; now reduced to herding sheep. Georgia had tried and tried again to explain, a Western District merino stud is not a shepherd in the Auvergne. *"Tant Pis,"* she'll never get it.

Georgia's parents Earn and Shirl fly in from London, British Airways to Bordeaux looking exactly what they are travelling Australians. In moleskin pants and riding boots, (R.M.Williams naturally) Akubra hat and merino suit made in Milano from their own wool. A tall man deeply tanned more bald than silver and while he has an Aussie twang he can soften it at will courtesy of time spent in Milano, London and Hong Kong. Dearest Shirl she stepped right up with the best of Chilton French. It's not too bad and not too good, muddles tenses and pronouns but what the heck and what the hell!!! At her best Shirl is full of pluck. Georgia's mum has dragged the farm from good to very good to best exactly as it should have been. "That's the job of wives'," she says. Although Georgia would not agree, it's not the job of wives' to be in the background when husbands shine. Even now Shirl's doing it putting her husband in the best of lights.

Shirl doesn't need to this is the man who taught Georgia how to ride a dirt bike through Western district mud, drive a tractor, round up sheep, fix a fence and hang a gate taught her how to crutch a sheep, cut off balls and shear the beasts. He is measured on a different scale, he don't need to impress La Countess imagine her if roles reversed, La Countess ankle deep in shit!

Georgia got her way just once, about the cellar, the ballroom wasn't big enough for so many rag-tag *Australiens!*

Georgia showed her daddy through the cellar being cleaned by Claude, ancient cellar master Chateau Haut Rivage cleaned first time in generations of dirt and dust and cellar mold. Just as Georgia planned it should for her to do what Georgia wants as the wife of Phillippe make her own Chateau Haut Rivage. Philippe had told her forcefully, "we have a cellar master, and a cellar master's son, they take care of everything we are a banking family."

Georgia replied, it looks like "FUN" Fun in capitals in fact and not in French that word is too long and spoken in an Aussi twang adding to the danger. A danger Phillip was aware he knew Georgia better than he is ever given credit for. Phillippe told Henri, his best man, on his and Georgia's wedding day.
"My wife to be you understand, is in love with my chateau as much or even more than me." It was a line, a throw away, it wasn't true at least not then, not today, no not today, her Cinderella moment.
Georgia Best in white (why not?) her bridesmaids both in flaxen straw Megs and Dot. Dot in spite of what she said about marriage and this marriage in particular. "It's not about Phillippe totally, it's marriage I'm objecting to. But I've spread my bullshit far and wide done and dusted let's enjoy your day and gosh, don't you look grand" In white lace strung with silver bead, blonde hair tied in ringlets a silver head piece a bloody tiara. "Who is the countess now I ask?"
"She always was a looker," Mathew summarized.
Megs in flaxen yellow dress, the sun-dried meadows of Haut Pyrenees. Megs is honeysuckle. Georgia Best a sorbet ice, cool with sparkling edges. Georgia beaming as she walks the aisle on her father's hand today minus his Akubra. A bittersweet day for the man who had hoped his daughter would marry a local lad, a good family from Geelong, Hamilton or Warrnambool, but, but, but, he'd always known she had wanted something more, something bigger, grander, than his world. Ernest Best, call me Earn was neutral about the French although Shirl likes them well enough. Earn has an uncle

buried here in the mud of Villiers-Bretonneux, today he wears his medals in respect on his left side jacket a minor statement which won't be lost, not on Grandfather Albert de Courmartin the old patriarch who silently and solemnly embraces him.

They say, "I do."

"I do."

And let's begin the feasting.

The cellar has been emptied, cleaned enough, a dance floor constructed between the casks, the band plays Waltzing Matilda.

The first wine served a Cadillac forever will be on the list, (of the Lost Great Wines Mathew & Flinders Wine Merchants) on Georgia Best's say so. The wine a cousin to Barsac, to Sauternes on the better side of river. The Cadilac is neither as lush nor as sweet, thus is more an aperitif, apricot and citrus peel, honeysuckle, herbs and spice. Clink a glass of Cadillac, Georgia Best and Megs and Dot, "to the future and to us." The Cadillac, they follow up with a Chateau Haut Rivage, dry white Graves (almost but it isn't) "A perfect illustration of everything the Chateau is," Her father-in-law pronounced that day. In the sweet bliss of the day Georgia could taste it all, the restrained fruit, chalky tannins framing it and something else, the mystery, majesty of its own terroir.

Mathew thought the very same but flipped about, flipped upside down, Australian's in their naive way place fruit above the stuff French love; tannin, oak and something else. Mathew thinks but doesn't say. This wine is crying out for fruit, and that thinks Matt is the truth. Matty sees what Matty sees, his private way of seeing, a muddy brown with a tinge of grey, not the colour in the glass that is golden, perfectly, no the colour he sees inside, in his stupid inner sight. It's just a colour, nothing more, a flash of colour, comes and goes and Matty prefers to ignore it, mostly, except just then, it contradicts the evocative words of Monsieur de Courmartin. The Cadillac has a sweetish spice, a lower harmony of orange peel, whereas the Chateau Haut Rivage white doesn't have that whimsical tone, it is just a little flat thinks Matt. He wonders if Georgia thinks the same, but not today, no not today.

A wedding waltz begins to play Georgia and Phillippe danse elegantly while Mathew searches amongst the tables for one more bottle of Cadillac.

Another wine upon the list, the list not yet invented. A perfect wedding wine to drink at this most perfect wedding.

37
They named the bloody wine "Juliet"

Pierre La Blanc understands where he stands within this world his father held this job before, his grandfather before his father did. "We have our ways. We understand our Terroir and how to make Chateau Haut Rivage the way it always has been. We are," he says to his son Clive, "custodians of the Chateau wine."

Clive La Blanc listened to his father Pierre as he did to his old grandfather and had he still been alive he'd have listened to his great grandfather. Did that mean he must accept, all the old ways, it did not. Clive La Blanc was the first La Blanc to attend the University against his father's disregard. "Winemaking can only be taught in the cellar!" Piere spoke with authority. And yet, even Peire was not blind to what is happening all around Bordeaux. The family Chateau's under siege from Paris money and new ideas. (There are families selling up, there are new wines in wine shops who once only stocked their own, he knew the world was changing.)

Phillippe's gorgeous new wife charmed the boy, of course, he weren't a boy, he was roughly the same age as her. "It is not a big thing," Clive told Peirre, "one small patch, one hectoliter, nothing more, and a tank to store it in."

"Americans store wine in steel," Pierre remarked, "Industrial" for emphasis.

A stainless-steel tank came from Turino Italy. The first one in the cellar.

"I don't want to store my wine in wood," Georgia stated firmly, especially old wood" Complete with de Courmartin family crest and motto, (the Best family motto embossed on a water cart; "good, better, best, never let it rest, until your good is better and your better, best".) Georgia underlined the "Family" with a subtle roll of eye.

During the first vintage, Juliet was an embryo.

During the second an annoyance.

"I helped in the third." Juliet insisted.

By the third vintage, the one Juliet "helped in" Georgia rounded out the edges of the dry white Semillon she was making. Georgia stopped using the old crusher which she thought wasn't delicate enough for the whites. It battered the fruit too much between the destemmer prongs, the rollers and the open throated must pump screws. Georgia decided to by-pass it entirely and load full bunches in the press. Yes, it wasn't the best press an old wooden basket racket press and although the stalks might crush a bit, release a little, bitter stalk tannin. Georgia was certain, "if we are gentle, gentle Clive we can keep it all in check."

Piere naturally has explained the traditional process. The grapes from the vineyard are crushed into the press, fermented in the wooden casks then racked off into older barrels. The dry white Semillon is not an important wine. It is not the wine of the Chateau. In fact, it's lowly status is the reason why Georgia and Clive are allowed to make any at all. Pierre is unhappy, "Too much disruption," Pierre says, "vintage is hard enough without the extra work, extra picking days, even more to think about, even more to organize and an extra pressing day or two. Georgia promises they will do everything, but everything is never all. Disruption breeds disruption.

Georgia Best can see it now in retrospect, that wonderous thing. (Without forgiving Phillippe of his obstinancy of his famous Frankish "NO" it's their cultural privilege when you are perfect what's to change?) It is the dilemma at the heart of all the world's lost wines how to preserve and modernize, how to improve and yet not lose? How to bring along the folk whose heart and soul is in this wine? She found an ally in the son Clive but at the cost of the two, Pierre and Phillippe's (the two "P's"she called them, in a pod.) Georgia would put up with their if not quite antagonism at the very least, a grumbling acquiescence of the "silly wife's" new hobby.

Georgia and Clive picked their fruit before the main vintage had begun, picked, and placed it in the press. Pressing gently for a softer juice extraction at the cost of yield, which is not a problem on their scale, or not to them at the very least. Philippe, had never known the girl who'd climbed the gantry of Great Western wines who'd worked the hoses, lugged about the pumps, jumped inside fermenters. The Georgia Best of marc and shit.

Philippe barely recognized her. He knew the Paris lawyer not this girl with babe slung on back bent picking fruit. The babe who picked fruit from year one.

"I had a baby, made a wine, set two things upon the globe. I dragged hoses, set up pumps, scrubbed out tanks and cleaned out marc. I changed nappies, breastfed babe, in the vineyard, in the cellar, at the press. I conceived them both. I had a vision (don't tell Matt) of the wine I'd like to make of the daughter I will have. (I hate his spooky vision thing) And anyway, neither is exactly what I envisioned them to be." Georgia would one day explain to Juliet.

"Go on say it mum"

"Juliet the wine and you are both an enigma to me."

Georgia's wine had a rocky start, a turbulent adolescence. Georgia did not name the wine that was Phillippe in her honour actually. Or so he said but not once explained in whose honour it was named.

Georgia continued to explain, "Once a year and only once, did I get to make my wine. Once a year I could correct whatever I thought I didn't do as well as I could the year before. Except it is a different year perhaps, it was warmer, wetter, drier, windier, cloudier. The Gods of weather have their say, that's the curse of farming. It's not a reason to do the same, sorry to the two P's but it's just not. It is a reason to try to be more adaptive, flexible, more imaginative in what we do, Wine is easy in the best of years they allow us to bumble through it's the poor years which expose our inadequacies, it's when we need to use our brains, our knowledge, our imagination. We cannot make last vintage wine and make it so much better; we have to make the wine we have, that's our curse and challenge."

Juliet was strapped upon her back, bundled up in down cocoon. Georgia Best the peasant wife, she laughed remotely to herself. "If you want to play at vigneron, vigneron is what you'll be." Secateurs in winter wind, chill wind ruffling from low dark cloud, white tops waves on the broad estuary, a willy-willy wind which sweeps water reeds and river trees, stings her cheeks and hands once gloves are saturated in dampish air. Wouldn't call this rain or mist, wouldn't call it anything, except uncomfortable, Georgia thought, for her, for babe, she won't stay long. She will prune a row perhaps begin the next as well. She will come back tomorrow and the next, a row a day will do it girl.

She would show them all that she is made of tougher stuff than they believe. Georgia hadn't realized how cold and damp and dark that Bordeaux winters are.

Juliet being breastfed milk and sap, breastfed secateurs, vineyard rows and Bordeaux rain which will turn to sleet some days, occasionally will turn to snow. Spring storms before a warm and humid summer rarely hot. "What we would call hot", Georgia tells Juliet. Juliet will stand up grab a leaf, a twig, low hanging bunch, stand on tiptoes, naked girl, crunch the fruit and spit it out, while Georgia thought she was tasting fruit she was actually tasting sour. Juliet mouth an acid meter expressed in "Goo" or "Gaa" for every calibration. A calibration Georgia and Clive agree could be better, could be worse, not about to make a wine on a babies "Goo" or "Gaa." Even if they named the wine after their baby acid meter.

Thef ourth Juliet wine will be a great improvement on those before. A benign summer almost hot, hot enough to spend some time at La Plage, Atlantic coast. Philippe at his best relaxed away from banking world in the cool Atlantic swells which curve around the islands. Philippe in his summer shorts, summer shirt and summer hat, a Panama, it suits him well. A French summer they love to sit on the terrace eating fruit de Mer, drinking a chilled Muscadet sur Lie. Philippe claims, "a perfect match for fresh seafood."

"My Juliet could be as well imagine drinking our own wine."

Meanwhile Juliet herself wriggles on her mother's lap curious of this and that; a spoon, a serviette a shell, taking off her smart French hat.

"I guess our girl's Australian."

Philippe laughed trying to appreciate the woman beneath her perfect French who is something more and something else. He cannot exactly explain it to, himself, let alone someone else.

38
Chance Encounters Pilat Plage

An Australian couple, you can hear them speak, on a distant table, travelling south in campervan, struggling with the menu. Georgia says, "my countrymen, only Australians would ever sit on the furthest table. European's would sit nearby, and anyway I can hear them talk."

It's not a pronounced Australian "strine" but the twang is there. She invites them over, what the hell, it's been a while since she has spoken Oz.

Grant Chester (Shore Boy) and Michelle (SCEGS of course, same school as Dotty) a quick escape from London life, Barkley's Bank trading desk. He is exactly what he is Sydney elite personified from the best schools, best suburbs a stint in London have a ball. They are on their way south to Biarritz an Aussi short board in their van.

"At home I prefer a mini-mal I guess I'm just old fashioned."

Georgia Best understands the vocabulary of boys who surf; home means his "Home surf break" which is on the mid north coast where the "olds" have "hols."

"We learnt to surf on a left-hand shore break."

Phillippe listening understands as much as Jules, "Olds" and "Hols" and "Gromets" "Goofy foot" and "Left hand Break" and the banter of public schools. He does however understand this seriously handsome Australian man is outrageously flirting with his wife who reciprocates enthusiastically with an infant on her knee. An animation he hasn't seen, for years, no he has never seen, not that relaxed, not with that ease.

"Golly how I've missed it, just sort of raving on in Oz. My French is good but not as fun. Join us, join us lets us share a beer and seafood, and shoot the moon."

Michelle agrees it seems she is tired of "bum on towel" watching waves and Grant on board. Michelle thought she do more than sit on beach. She had visions of a shopping spree along the Champs Elysees not in the backwash of Breton. "I'd rather be in London."

"We ain't together you might have guessed, Grant is fun, well not this trip."

Grant and Georgia will have a beer but not so Philippe nor Michelle, she has a Frenchman, a handsome one, he owns a Chateau of course he does, knows the secret world of wine which he will share over this fragrant wine a Muscadet sur Lies from Nantes. "Oh, we surfed there, remember Elle, the break I said was a little like our Cactus."

Grant is flirting outrageously with the wife of Phillippe. The Australian girl, who he says dabbles in the cellar. Michelle looks at Georgia but doesn't see a girl who dabbles at anything. A familiar figure, Head Girl at whatever school (You can name them on two hands) Team Captain of Tennis, maybe hockey, she has that body which spent its youth playing sport competitively. Michelle admired the female form perhaps much more than she thought she should. She blamed school and changing rooms and too much of her life away from boys. A silly thought she shoves aside, Georgia truly does have lovely hair.

Michelle returns to handsome man wondering what it would be like to have a French lover, a cliché, in the end a man's a man and France, no not for her. Frenchmen do not travel, do not live in foreign lands not in Vaucluse, Sydney harbour side but today, today is fun, drinking wine on terrace not freezing on some dam French beach.

Engage, engage, in here and now, Michelle with the whiplash mind. Taste the wine, the Frenchman says.

"Lemon, lime and tropical, is that a hint of coconut?" Tastes she knows from someplace else, tastes of summer, Bondi beach. Michelle wonders how a wine can open up a memory, a place, a time, a snapshot of, a coconut summer, in red bowed hat with Bronwyn Murphy, Irish lass, black sprung hair, alabaster skin, smeared in coconut oil the smell of Aussi summer. Michelle's whiplash mind whips round again and back to here and back to now as conversation turns from wine to banking, common ground, money, trade and contracts.

"Contracts, what a bugbear, we need good lawyers on our side."

"Georgia is the best, you know."

"Well, I'll be, I'm not surprised."

The first of many, many lies. Grant was not surprised she's good but didn't understand the jest, implicit in the statement. Didn't know her name was Best, thought her name would now be French.

Georgia missing home today, an Aussie beach, underneath

umbrellas or on the deck of the Couta Yacht Squadron pretty much her favourite place. Georgia Best relaxing, the one thing she is not good at. (Thank you Matt for reminding me.) And even if it was a tease Grant Chester gave Georgia a card, "just in case, you never know, you might like to do some legal work in London. It's a pretty short commute, an hour's flight on British Air."

"You never know," Georgia Best repeated. She didn't know, and that's the truth, but even then suspected one day she might, what, need something to exercise the intellect she's famous for. Earning real money, do something, escape the confines of what she knows is just another provincial life. A distant and so difficult thought to let rattle in her head. Swirl about on winter wind, particularly that winter wind ruffling up the waters.

Georgia didn't leave for London then, that was so much, much latter. It was never supposed to be for good and actually it wasn't. It was all so reasonable, a chance for Georgia to return to English Common Law, not wallow in French bureaucracy.

39

I was there I tell you (Present minus 16 months)

Juliet would say to her friend Martinique, "As a feminist I agree she needed something of her own. The wine was not enough for Georgia and it came with just too many strings, all the family tensions, the family fights. Yes, I missed her but as she said, it was a short commute and she returned on weekends, most, holidays. In-between I had Gran, I had Dad and I had my little ecole. Mum away, gave my Gran, space to be a real Gran, Gran and I lived in the kitchen."

Juliet, (Always Juliet in France) loved that kitchen life with Gran, "La Countess" was not "La Countess" for Juliet, she was her French grandmother. Juliet loved the "science" of making, baking, mixing, bicarbonate of soda will froth and splutter in vinegar. The chemistry of taste, the everyday chemistry of the bench, yeast, and sugar, salt. The many acids of the world; some which tingle, they are the best, some which burn, don't touch those, some which heighten another sense, counterpoint and harmony. Juliet's French childhood was mostly good especially in summer on Atlantic coast, a week of winter in the Pyrenees, mum would always join us. Paris weekends Montmartre, on the tiny funicular. And always vintage in Bordeaux.

"Let me tell you, my mother's wrong, my mother cannot be trusted. I don't mean with daily things, pick you up from ballet or take you to the dentist. Georgia cannot be trusted with the truth, it's a lawyer thing, stick to the brief and nothing more. Truth is important, at least to me, the truth about my father. Georgia's analysis of love and loss is not her usual dispassionate, precise, and balanced self. No, she wants to prove she's right, right to leave him, in the way she did which are two different arguments which she mixes up. Georgia lives in the future tense while French has too many pasts for that."

Juliet has strong opinions of which she shares with Martinique, French girl from the Jura (what would Grandma think of that). Juliet's friend, perhaps lover, perhaps not. She wants her to know the truth of it, just the truth and nothing else. The story of Chateau Haut Rivage; the wine which her mother made which her mother likes to claim Juliet has no knowledge of.

"You weren't there," she likes to say,

"Where was I then?" Juliet counters.

"You were too young."

"Too young to what?" Understand, I never did, feel betrayed, I felt some things didn't have the words for them, still don't, if the truth be known. And we are talking truth today.

Juliet's father's French it comes as a package you don't get to choose the things you like and things you don't. "My father's French, and French has weight. The weight of history in a family rooted to a place, rooted to a purpose. Do not be the one to break that eternal chain. It is not eternal nothing is and only feels a chain sometimes. My father didn't want to be anything but that kind of Frenchman to respect tradition yet even he would feel occasionally the constraints of his culture, class, of his "Ancient Family."

Juliet de Courmartin always her pedantic self replied, "All families are ancient dad, pretty much by definition."

Her father's only true revolt was to marry Georgia. Her mother never understood Phillippe, "La Countess" or the French as much as she thought she did. "Understood the language, "Yes" it's not the same as understanding who they are. My mother speaks the language perfectly, far better than me", says Juliet. Juliet's French is always muddied up with all sorts of schoolgirl slang.

"My friend Onna likes to claim, she was conceived in the Pyrenees. It's why we are "sympatico", she says, curiously in Italian, of all the things we tell each other it really is the cutest lie." Juliet explains to Martinique.

Onna befriended Jules in school, usually in inverted commas, "School" that's better, Onna, Madison and Jules the oddballs at that bloody "School." Chilton Grammer school where Juliet bordered while Georgia was away, somewhere or everywhere.

"Oh one last thing" says Juliet to the beautiful Martinique, "My mother says that dad was always against her making wine. Dad says that he wasn't. He simply told her, "ask Pierre", he may have said it in a grump but not the way my mother thought. My Dad was not against her in anything. Their relationship is proof to me that her understanding of the French is sort of only language deep. It's why I like to speak French bad, my French is more French than hers can be because of all my badness."

40
Couta Boat Yacht Club deck (Autumn present minus 12 Months)

Mathew and Georgia begin to plan an autumnal dinner, post-harvest, Mathew's small harvest of Amarone Shiraz. His final link to a passed life.

The bay is calm what Megs would call a pastel grey and Mathew "tourmaline" except Megs is not here Georgia is.

Megs would normally help Mathew plan their dinners, but this dinner is at Georgia's thus Georgia is helping. They are sipping a Claire Valley Riesling (Polish River).

"We can't put it on the list, it's not quite lost, thank God for that."

Georgia has her hair pinned back. She is wearing blue jeans and a stylish shirt and sits squarely in her seat. Georgia does not place her feet upon an adjacent chair. Georgia has no sketchpad balanced on her knee. Georgia's hair does not cascade from beneath her summer hat, nor does she smile a secret smile for Matt alone. It is not the same and yet there is an easiness between the two of them born of long time knowing. Born of Georgia knowing Matty adores her and always has and because Matty has become the person which he has complete with wine shop and our eccentric Society.

"Having the dinner at my place will give Megs a chance to just be a guest. No kitchen chores, no serving guests, no plates or drinks, just relax."

A nice gesture Mathew thought if not without a touch of; "one up girl ship."

Mathew knew Georgia thought Mathew's first and last dinner a haphazard affair. Mathew thought that dinner relaxed. Georgia thought that dinner too relaxed. Georgia's dinner would be the "Best." She had organized it in her head. The theme is French, naturally, although in truth she is thinking Aquitaine. A nod to Chateau Haut Rivage, to La Countess, and her fractured past.

"We can pour a Bordeaux Grand Cru, (Bordeaux at its best) a wine to please Travis Loyd. Travis, Georgia reminds Mathew, is suppost to be my boyfriend. Travis will be there, and I still think, he could be useful to your shop.

Mathew, Georgia, both know it is complicated. Travis is Georgia's present boyfriend. He is rich, English, snobbish. Travis is a good match for Georgia's public self. Georgia's corporate lawyer self, for the life Georgia admits she is tired of, mostly finished with, perhaps not good a match for Georgia's Fairhaven self. Relaxing on the deck of the Couta Yacht Squadron sipping Riesling and slurping oysters. Matty musing all things wine and all things come and gone. Musing over all the might have beens. "Mister Time Warp" looking back. Mathew is musing the loss of Meg's faith in him and the might have, could have beens. If he had just been what? Less naive, better at "covering his arse," better at the corporate game, a little more like Travis. No, he couldn't be a Travis and Georgia wouldn't want him to be. Georgia Best wants Mathew just to be Mathew.

Georgia worked in the corporate world, knows what you need to survive and Matty nearly, nearly did and then did not. "Tant Pis" she says returns to French. The wine shop suits him, a good fit, his ancestors business after all. Even if he wasn't born with the name he wishes. He is not a Leske, never was. Truth was he wouldn't have lost as much if he hadn't tried to be what he wasn't. Georgia laughs a private laugh, "but then my daughter says lawyers wouldn't know the truth if they fell over it." Georgia says but only to herself.

41

Plans and Preparation

An autumn dinner will take place once they pick Mathew's Shiraz. The not quite Amarone allowed to dry upon the vine, raisined slightly in autumn sun. His wine is a homage to sun and straw, a sparkling red wine, he first helped make in Great Western.

Jules has come the day before to requisition Mum's kitchen. "A nod to La Countess," Juliet says, "I learnt to cook on Grannies knee, and I am about to amaze you all."

Jules arrived with Martinique, "her dish pig", they have a plan. They have brought everything they need. "Mum would have had it catered but we can do much better."

Georgia suspects there is a hint of "fuck you," in Jules being with Martinique, or so she tells Mathew."

Georgia shrugging, "she is navigating more lives than one. I would prefer she marry an Australian boy." Echoing the thoughts of Earn who had said similar things to her, marry a Western District boy, that's what Dot did in her way."

Jules bonded with the Jura girl presumably over their appalling French. Georgia suspects they bang it on just as she and Dotty did, exaggerating an outback dust filled drawl. The girl is pretty in a wildling way as the country from which she came, red haired, freckles, wild loose hair. The Jura is a different France Georgia doesn't know at all although surprisingly Dotty does. They make wines in the Jura as untamed as their county side, rustic wines full of tangled briny fruits, porcini mushroom, forest debris, wild herbs. Baz would love them. Baz's wines also taste as his countryside if not a little how he dresses and always has. The wine is the winemaker, written large. Generally, Georgia don't agree, it's the "Terroir" but not is seems in every case sometimes the personality of the winemaker creeping in just as Kato often says.

"This house is way to big for her." Juliet says to Martinique while standing before an expansive window looking out on ocean swell rise and fall below them. On the bluff, the ocean side of the headland on which the town is wrapped. . Mathew's house on lower cliffs facing the harbour, pier and boats riding bouys, the original town of Fairhaven. Newer houses around the bluff, Georgia's beach house amongst them.

"It's not a beach house," Juliet begins a diatribe to Martinique. "A beach house is all about the beach, there is a clue in the name which is lost on Mum. My friend Onna has a beach house, it is full of sand and towels, wetsuits drying on verandah rails. The kind of chaos which screams fun. My mother's beach house is a display, of what? For whom, I wouldn't know?"

"It's austere, and very white."

"I know she has plans for it. She has plans. She always does. She had plans for me which never quite materialized. I weren't the daughter she planned to have."

Martinique took her hand and dragged her towards the kitchen.

"A modern kitchen I understand. Let us unpack provisions. All we need to do tonight is marinate the beef. We have all day tomorrow."

Not all day, they both know that, for they will wake up mid-ish morn then to the beach with Onna.

42

North Head Beach Late Morning Saturday

"It's a good swell. Or so says Jake but what would I know," Onna says to Jules and Martinique laying on the North Head beach. "Waves are waves, I used to think, but I kind of get it. I appreciate the way they curve around the point it has a clinker hull kind of feel."

Jake has left an old mini-mal surfboard on the beach for them to use Onna suggests, "we should try. Come on Jules, let's have some fun!"

Jules' non-committal looks out to seaward pondering the sine and cos of ocean swell, frequency and amplitude.

Martinique has the broadest grin. "I am on a bloody Australian beach, my chance to be a surfy chick. Let's go. Let's do it. Let's have some ocean fun."

"You go Onna, Martinique, my mum says Onna don't be Michelle. Cryptic, yes, I know it is. Some Aussi girl she once knew her sat on towel why her friend surfed all along the Atlantic coast. Don't sit on towel, don't be that girl bring out your inner Goldie."

Jules is sitting bum on towel while Onna, Martinique and board splash in shore wash, shore foam, tumbling wave break on the beach. Washing up across the sand falling back and then again. No mere ripple on the sea, these waves are nearly the size of them. Waves which lift the board and Martinique and hurl them back to where they began. They try and try again, Onna succeeds in dragging both board and Martinique beyond the shore break to quieter waters, between the shore break and the reef further out where Jake is paddling before a wave. Martinique clasped to the board is washed back shoreward. "That was fun."

Onna's turn, she tries to squat on the wildly dancing board. It flicks her over the next turn.

"Okay I am asking Goldie."

Jake "hangs-five" or some such thing, neither knowing what that means, as he rides a wave to shore. "Smart-arse bastard," Onna greets her boy.

Jake says, "Hi," to Juliet, " I hear you are chef tonight. I'll tell you now. I am starving."

"Well maybe I should just run off, to the kitchen, a woman's place."

Martinique insists they don't she wants to try just one more time, to do something on that bloody board."

Onna appraising the mini-mal, says, "If I made a bigger board with gunnels perhaps but then it sort of becomes a boat."

"You could make yourself a board," Jake tells Onna enthusiastically, "surfboards were once made of wood before everyone turned to fiberglass."

"I could make a surfboard Jake. But first, I would need to learn to surf. Feel exactly what a board knows about the ocean."

"Jules", says Jake, "I am only joking girl. Not about starving but that you ought be going back to cook."

"We should be soon but not just yet. Jake why don't you take out Martinique she wants to be a surfy chick. Show her how to get passed the shore break. How to stay on just enough to have surfy kind of fun. And don't worry about the food, the food will be great, homage to this land and sea."

43
An Autumnal Dinner

First course will be "Fruit de Mer." Tiger prawns, Coffin Bay oysters, Tasmanian salmon in a finger lime and mango sauce. Matched with Jule's "Juliet."

"Juliet, named for me and made by Dad, I helped as well. Mum made it first, and Best she'll say."

"And I did," Georgia trumpets.

The evening a perfect autumn eve, warm and clear, the ocean beyond Georgia's vast window a nearly perfect turquoise blue fading slowly into gun tint grey. Jake and Goldie staring out into the swell lines around the heads. "I was there today," he gestures to the breaking surf, "It was good, a little chop but it is always good to get wet."

Goldie smiles, thinking much the same as Jake.

"Onna tried to surf today, first time, worst time, thinks she ought ask you for some pointers."

"And you won't help her?"

"I think she would prefer to hear it from a girl."

"Not from her boyfriend, smart arse bloke. Makes perfect sense I'll let her know when I go out."

Goldie looked back towards the sea. "I love this light. This time of day. The seeping together of sea and sky. The slow fade, the night begins."

He stands, she stands. Jake is not a man of many words but has Mathew's ease of being. An easy man to stand and look when you have no expectations.

Megs can't help herself once the light begins to fade. Once the colours turn to grey, once the dining room lights begin over shadowing sea and sky. She turns to the kitchen to help Jules and her French friend Martinique.

"Your seafood platter is glorious and the sauce "to kill for." What is that flavour?"

"Finger lime."

"Georgia told me you loved to cook. I didn't realize you were this good."

"Well let's serve up, after all, the proof is in the eating."

Seafood platter, fruit de mer, served with Juliets own "Juliet" dry white Bordeaux, a semillon.

It's not her wine anymore. Georgia can see Philippes touch or Philippes wine consultants touch. Georgia's wine was more austere, tight, it had a zing, this wine has lost the zing. This "Juliet" is broader in the palate with richer fruits tastes and a warmer feel. This "Juliet" is much more welcoming, a friendly version of the wine. It is less edgy and therefore less like the daughter it was named for and that thinks Georgia is a pity.

"Beautiful citrus, lemon, lime, grassy herbs and passionfruit," says Goldie, "and I taste a lick of oak. Overall, a modern wine and yet not one which I would make." Goldie favours the austere style. As does Baz but Mathew says, "Commercially it makes more sense, I could sell a ton of this." Echoing Two-Stroke who simply says, "This wine delightful, thank you Jules."

Zak finds Jules a quandary, the wine they named after her is not really her at all. It is too safe for a girl who says pretty much anything which pleases her. Goldie, who Zak admires the most, the only one he'd listen too. Goldie is a fan of Morrissey after all. Is hesitant to dismiss the wine. "I appreciate what they are trying to do."

Georgia understands, Philippe couldn't make Georgia's wine. He needed bring it into line with Chateau Haut Rivage's style, keep it in the family.

While Jules defends her father's wine (and Her's) "A wine is not an exclamation mark. It doesn't need to say something. A wine is not a message in a bottle. It needs be sound (chemically) and as Dad says, "Be viable in the marketplace."

"Ah the banker," Georgia says, "I am sorry Jules, but your father wouldn't be Philippe without his viable in the marketplace."

"Surprisingly I agree," says Baz, "both with your assessment of the wine and Philippe's of his marketplace. A good wine must do many things and one of them is pay the bills."

Travis doesn't think the wine is worthy of discussion. The marketplace that's something else, "a wine like this, without a cru, with barely appellation must make money, why else make it after all."

"Oh my God," screams Helena, "An artist doesn't compromise! Ever! If there is something you want to say, then bloody well just say it." Or scream it in an accented voice which carries the judgement of another land, the Prague Spring circa 1968.

Zak is just as adamant. Zak is just as certain, "and a wine is exactly that, a message in a bottle! Ho-hum, ho-hum we don't need more, ho-hum wines. You don't see Goldie making wine to please anyone except herself."

"Thank you, Zak, but it's not true. Goofy-foot Wines must pay its way. Lucky for me just enough people like my wines."

It ought to be simple but it's not. Zak is right and Zak is wrong. Wine is more than passion and wine is naught without it.

"Talking of passion," says Goldie, "I want to complement our chief, this seafood platter and the sauce is as delightful as the wine. If I can I'd like us to break with France for a moment to introduce not just a wine but a label brought to you by Madison Golightly."

They will open a Goldie's Grenache, artwork by Madison Golightly, grapes grown their own Baz. A family wine if there ever was. Homage to Spain to Spanish soils, homage to Baz's Navarre soils, homage to Miro who Maddy loves to sun and soil and Pyrenees. You can see it all a joyous riot of squiggles, blobs of colour, and landscape.

"I adore it," Helena screams, "it's so Madison and so much more. Beauty is what you bring the world. And every act of beauty is an act of courage darling girl."

Two-Stroke, who has watched the label emerge, smiles a smile of true delight. "It's gorgeous Maddy, it has a buzz, a spark, a bang! It's the package Maddy girl." (It's a Honda full throttle out on the highway of your dreams) He can see it all. Goldie's story by itself is great, what she's done with Baz's fruit is fab, but the label, cream on top. It captures the essence of our times, moving in and moving out of a wave break of the past, traditional viticulture, new wave wine. He knows that Madison doesn't think like him but here is a wine which will sell itself in edgy inner suburbs.

Madison's right about the "GLAM" she has brought the "GLAM" to Goldie's wine. And brings the "GLAM" to Mathew's nights. As does Helena and Reggie too, singing their light Opera. Let's not forget that wine is fun. Wine is celebration. Roll out the barrels, pull out the corks, laugh and joke and sometimes take it seriously.

Goldie winks at Two-Stroke from across the table. "You were right." The wink says, "Not that I ever doubted."

Georgia asks Travis what he thinks of the artwork and the wine. Knowing the answer, but what the heck.

"They are I think a good match, surprisingly I agree with your Japanese friend, well marketed I could see this wine make Goldie a good profit. Not my taste but interesting, I know some French winemakers doing this, ignoring the appellation rules to make a different product. Edgy as he says, perfect inner-city wine for the bars where I tend not eat except with you occasionally.

Reggie watching Two-Stroke work the room on Maddy's behalf. "It's not a given," he whispers low, to Helena, just to her, "that we even recognize who we need at our side and who is our sympatico."

"I think however," Reg says to Helena, "that Onna, gets it, or gets it enough. Jack the surfer is a handsome man in that mode of surfer boys hanging out on Skinners corner. Talking of reef breaks, talking of girls and getting out of this small town. Except Jake is ruled by lessor gods, those of small ambition. All he wants is to work with plants, fine by him. Find a girl, live a life, just an ordinary life ocean life."

Onna chats with Siobahn while wine folk talk of tannins, describing them in lush, lush words.

They talk of their equivalent. "Sometimes I wish that I could taste all the things they talk about. What I taste is wineness, can't pull apart the threads of wine only the grains of timber."

"Sometimes I wish that I could see it too but not enough it's their world. I have my Kato. I am not jealous of Kato's wine."

Georgia taps her glass bringing attention back to. "It's time to return to the theme of our night which is France but France as witnessed by Australian eyes. Australian/French eyes if you will. Juliet will serve for you a slow cooked beef with lemon myrtle, pepper, cummin and fennel with roast beetroot on a bed of saltbush leaves. The wines a Margaret River Bordeaux blend tasted blind against a true Bordeaux."

Mathew poured a glass of each just before the food was served to .

taste them naked, so to speak. Swirl about and take a breath. We will unmask them shortly.

Wine One; is classic cabernet, cigar box and cedar nose, dark berry, violet, tobacco leaf, silky tannins, a rich wine, dense, intense, explodes with fruit.

Wine Two; unmistakably Cabernet the nose is similar, classic cigar box and cedar wood but with an underfloor of forest floor. Wine two has more pronounced spice and herb a subtler wine, more subdued, and yet richer in a unique way than wine one which Travis calls "Flashy very parvenue."

Wine two is French they all agree. In fact a Chateau Beychevelle. Wine one a Cullen Cabernet, Margeret River, Western Australia.

"What is different? What is the same?" That's the question in Mathew poses. "Same cigar box nose within a cedar frame yet wine two has something else, a hint of river mud perhaps a subtle nuance of countryside. Of course, the blend is not quite the same the Margeret River has more Cabernet then the Chateau Beychevelle. I think that is the least important. The difference in my eyes at least is in the purity of fruit reflected in the Cullen wine."

Georgia adds, "I think the Cullen, Margeret River wine is magnificent, clean, well balanced, subtle tannins and remarkable subtle wood. A beautiful rich fruit cake of taste but I return to the Chateau Beychevelle which has I think more layers to explore, therefore more interesting. And while I am not sure every layer is perfect; every layer says something more tells a complex story. I am of course a Francophile. The best of France can be divine which incidentally is why I detest her worst wine. Oh! It could be much better."

"As a Franc," Juliet emphasized the lack of "phile", "I concur, my mother's right. My mother hated inferior Bordeau, my father shrugged and always said, 'so long as we don't make it.' Which brings us to our main course today. Slow cooked beef with lemon myrtle, cummin, fennel with roasted beetroot on a saltbush bed. Enjoy!"

Served by Megs and Martinique, she wasn't supposed to be doing that.

"But which is better with the meal? Jules poses the obvious, "now I have biased it with all my native flavours."

"Your ever so delightful meal has unfairly biased the way I see both wines," says Mathew, "or simply reinforced my prejudice. I prefer the Margeret River wine, it's rich flavours complement the beef, the salt bush leaves, a nice touch Jules, reflected in the hint of ocean present in the Cullen wine."

Georgia is not so sure how Mathew can be definitive. "Chateau Beychevelle has layers upon layers of intriguing, nuanced subtleties the Cullen dense fruit flavours. And while my daughters Australian spice marries with the Cullen wine to me the Cullen is slightly less for lacking in dimensions. A self-confessed Francophile goes with the territory don't you think."

Travis is definitive, "an Australian wine could never eclipse an appellation Bordeaux Grand Cru, end of the discussion."

Except it wasn't, not for Jules. "The dance of molecules does not deceive. It simply is and nothing more. Wine sponges up so many things. The smell of place, fragrance of trees, scent of flowers, phenols of grass, cypress oils and spearmint gums. Cellar damp and cellar moulds, oak is not a barrier to the air outside it nor are grape skins impermeable, they breath it in and breath it out. Breath in the history of the land. One smells so subtlety of ocean shore the other Gironde estuary. It is how it takes you back, the best of wine a time machine."

Kato ponders. Kato thinks. The strange girl does make sense tonight all part of a larger puzzle.

Mathew and Georgia discussing wine. Reggie discussing dinner, "I think our Jules has done us proud. The beef, the wines are magnificent. I haven't ate so well since ninety two."

No one bothered asking.

Pear tart and Monbazillac brings Jules dinner to conclusion, not of wine and not of life but of the serious discussion of either one or indeed of both. The simple sticky wine of Bergamot is more pleasure than a prompt.

Helena, however, has to chime right in, "we should be drinking our Tokay. Even if it was destroyed by the Soviets, scum of earth."

"Or the wines of Portugal" Kato and Goldie in unison, look at each with true surprise. They have never talked about it.

"I used to surf there."

"I used to work there."

"Where?"

"Where?"

Begins a conversation, while Siobhan talks to Megs about a painting on the kitchen wall done by Megs so long ago of the Megs in vineyard Chateau Haut Rivage.

"You have a talent. You have an eye."

"Two eyes." Says Megs whose blushing.

Reggie, Helena and his son Zak on the keyboards once again prepare to serenade the group with their opera buffa. H.M.A.S *Pinafore,* First Lord of the Admiralty.

"I am the Monarch of the sea
My gallant cru good evening
I am the Captain of the Pinafore
I command a right good crew
Give three cheers and one cheer more
For the haughty Captain of the Pinafore

I am the monarch of Couta boats
Not sure Georgia will come aboard
You will have to sing the chorus Matt
The three of us upon the sea
Give three cheers and one cheer more
For the haughty Captain of the Pinafore

We will take Kato of course we will
We will need a warrior of the sea
Siobhan will be our guide
Lovely silkie of the sea.
Give three cheers and one cheer more
For the haughty Captain of the Pinafore."

Georgia raised an eye at Matt, "You have just been told. It is your call mate."

44

I never quote Mathew (1st. person singular)

I never quote Mathew I find that's best. I am sorry Onna but he is the least rational of all of us, except the part where Mathew says something insightful about wine. Mathew says, he don't know why, grape varieties do not find an easy translation to foreign lands, nor sometimes do people. It is generational, they spent an inordinate amount of time debating the status of Australian wine and whether we should we always frame it by the classic wines of Europe. Cultural cringe and nothing else, we are internationalists. And yet it explains why Mathew made a sparkling Syrah his signature.

Me; I translate perfectly. I can step from Bordeaux to the beach. I like to say, but it's been said, rather nasty I would think that I am not a perfect fit in here or there. I speak perfect Argot French and bloody good Australian. I am half French, no matter what they say. Perhaps they are right enough you see; I do feel tugged between them.

Mathew says wine is like my tugging, every variety finds it hard to fit in foreign shores and foreign soils. Sometimes they can, sometimes they do, find a new expression of themselves. Sometimes they just act as though they had never really left their home. He was thinking of Travis who we don't like. Mum's Travis has never left England's green and pleasant land. Mathew is jealous, it is obvious to all of us. I just think Travis is a rather pompous version of the men my mother always has wrapped around her gorgeous arm.

Two families, two friendship groups, two languages, two cultures, two parts, two pulls, two purposes.

Look at Two-Stroke, he can't hide his Asian face a calling card. Even his name has "Two" in it.

Look at Kato who also wears his displacement on his skin.

Me, I play both, Mademoiselle and Aussie girl, bang it on occasionally, just as Mum does when she is with Dot.

It was a good dinner, by and large, left things hanging, things unsaid. Madison and Two-Stroke, I don't know. Kato's story, you need to know, Mathew and Meg's and Reggie too. Onna and Jack least of all, they will bumble on for sure (or shore). Small stories of our ordinariness. And more postcards on the wall.

"Let me tell you something more and not about my mother. There is a postcard on the wall, it's from me, I sent it. From the Jura, just to prove, I can play their silly game, it is in a sparkling "texta", but before I tell you that, there is something else worth knowing."

The postcard from the Jura was written with sparkling texta by Juliet.

Ungoverned France
Unruly France
Unkept Jura Hill side towns.

www.ingramcontent.com/pod-product-compliance
Lightning Source LLC
Chambersburg PA
CBHW030532020726
47494CB00004B/1330